THE YEAR OF GREATS

Marleen Kunze

ISBN: 1-953287-00-X
ISBN-13: 978-1-953287-00-7

I would like to thank my son Mike for getting my books published and my son Jeff for illustrating the covers of all three books.

I would like to thank my husband John for encouraging me to write each evening and for turning the sound down on the TV whenever I ask him to.

Thanks also to my friends Judy and Connie and my daughter Kerry, who read all of my books, and who edited and discussed this book with me.

I'm grateful for the Coronavirus, which gave me the time to write the last half of the book The Year of Greats.

Also By Marleen Kunze

The First Ten Days

In a moment, life changes forever...

Imagine a time when millions of people from every country in the world disappear off the face of the earth. Such an event can actually happen "in the twinkling of an eye," according to I Corinthians 15:52 and I Thessalonians 4:17. Marleen Kunze considers the impact that disappearances can have on an ordinary middle-class American family in *The First Ten Days*. Matt Moses and his family investigate his missing sister's family, and in the process, they live in their house, drive their cars, eat their food, and spend their money.

As the Moses family live the life of their missing family, will they enjoy the easy life, will they wish they too had disappeared, or will they take up the mission of their relatives? What evil forces will the family face in a world that changes dramatically in just The *First Ten Days*?

Escape From Rome

No good deed goes unpunished…

Go back to a time in history when the Roman Empire controlled most of the world. One hundred thousand men spent their days at the Coliseum and other arenas watching vicious animal performances.

In Marleen Kunze's *Escape From Rome*, the adventure begins when the Coliseum manager's teenage sons witness a bloody performance and rescue a man about to be trampled and gored by rhinos. The fateful rescue angers the emperor and endangers the lives of Nolan's entire family.

Fleeing from the ruthless Emperor Domition, a handful of teenagers join the hunting team Nolan sends to Africa. As they trek around the Great Sea, they search for wild animals, and find survival and the truth about God.

Will the family escape from Rome and find the Christian faith they realize they are seeking? Or will they be captured by the the emperor's men and sent into the arena?

For sample chapters, and information about upcoming books visit **https://marleenkunze.com**.

Chapter 1

It was on that worst night of her life, that the idea was born in Jenna's mind. *I don't have to take this anymore. I can run away and never see them again.* Hours before, as she sat in her room studying for an American history test, the phone rang, and her parents insisted that she walk across town and drive them home from their favorite bar. They were intoxicated, and they should not get behind a wheel.

Jenna put on her coat, opened the front door, and was greeted by a blast of freezing rain. Since her mom refused to buy her a decent pair of boots, Jenna had to wear her tennis shoes, which soaked in the icy water as she ran across the grass. When she stepped out onto the street, she hit the ice, and slid on her bottom, drenching her clothes. She got up and picked her way across block after block of ice-covered pavement, getting splashed occasionally as cars passed by. When she arrived at the bar, her feet, legs, and hands were numb, so she limped awkwardly, and the frozen strands of her hair stood out, making her resemble a troll.

On the drive home, Jenna's fingers were so stiff that she could barely hold the steering wheel. But it was her mother's words that sent a permanent chill through her body.

"I hope you are proud of yourself, Missy; humiliating us like that in front of our friends. Bursting into our favorite place, wind and rain gusting through the door, and you standing there looking like a crazed scarecrow. Now that is a scene I will remember forever," said Jenna's mother Cynthia through clenched teeth. "And what took you so long?"

Jenna knew there was nothing she could say that would appease her, so she just shrugged her shoulders. Her father was already snoring loudly on the seat next to her, a reminder that she will somehow have to get him into the house.

"Well answer me, you stupid girl," screamed her mother. The sound caused Jenna to stomp on the brake, sending the car into a spin. They hit the curb hard. A horn blasted nearby and her father flopped over on the seat. Her mother realized that she should keep quiet in order to arrive home alive. Jenna straightened the wheels and managed to get through town, reach their house, and pull into the garage. She helped her mother in first, and once inside, was given a slap on the face for embarrassing them in front of their friends. Her father was even meaner, calling her ugly and punching her in the back. After that night, Jenna never initiated a conversation or even a single word to either parent. From then on, she spent every waking moment planning her escape.

In the eyes of the public, Jenna's parents were model citizens. Her father was a famous lawyer and her mother was the mayor of their city. Most of the people they worked with thought they were responsible, dependable, and likable. Their dearest and closest friends, who drank with them, knew that they had a tendency to get drunk or high, but they were either like them or they were amused by them. But Jenna knew the real Harold and Cynthia Ashcraft.

Jenna's parents were evil on a good day, but when they drank, they punished her mentally and physically. They were always careful to hurt her in ways that didn't show.

Once, when Jenna was twelve, they were angry at her for spilling milk, so they dumped the rest of the carton in the sink, and didn't buy her milk for a long time. Usually they just hit her. They feared public embarrassment more than anything, so her parents carefully managed to stop before they left scars, physical ones at least. But after the night of the ice storm, her compliance turned to an obsession to disappear and not leave a trace.

Jenna had a homeroom teacher named Mrs. Nelson, who seemed to be really concerned about her. In fact, one time Mrs. Nelson asked her if she was abused. Jenna denied it, but always wondered if people could tell just by looking at her. Since the ice storm, Jenna wanted to confide in Mrs. Nelson. In fact, every time she walked by her classroom, Jenna thought about different things she could tell Mrs. Nelson. But teachers were probably required to report abuse, so Jenna decided to handle the problem on her own.

Jenna knew better than to research her escape on her parents' home computer. Every day after school, she went to libraries around town, searching for the perfect place to live. She considered Florida or Southern California due to the fact that the nights would not be quite as cold if she became homeless, and because there were probably thousands of runaways in those states already. She was also considering other countries, like Mexico or Canada, because they would be the last place anyone would look for her.

One day, discouraged and ready to go home, Jenna decided to go to the library's restroom. There on the door of the stall was a notice of help for battered women. They listed an eight hundred number. *I wonder if they could help battered teenage girls.* She copied down the number and went into the hall, where there was a pay phone. Jenna thought that at the least she could get some advice, so she punched in the numbers.

"Circle of Hope," answered the lady. "Can I help you?"

"I don't know where to start," Jenna answered.

"Are you, or someone you know, being abused, in any way?" the lady asked.

"Yes," answered Jenna. "It's me. I don't know what to do. I want to run away."

"You sound young," said the lady.

"I'm seventeen years old," Jenna answered.

"Is your father or step-father abusing you?" asked the lady.

"It's my father and mother. They despise me," Jenna said.

"Are you in immediate danger?" asked the lady.

"I never know. It depends on how much they've been drinking," Jenna answered.

"What do you want us to do for you?" asked the lady.

"I want to travel to a city far away, disappear, and never come back," said Jenna. "Can you do that for me?"

"We do have shelters in many cities, but it's tricky with teenagers. It usually takes a court order for us to place them somewhere," she said. "Social services will have to do an investigation and …."

Jenna hung up quickly because she knew that she would lose all freedom, if her parents thought she would discuss this stuff with anyone. She went back upstairs and looked at the computers. Jenna felt a funny feeling in her chest, like there was a void inside. She was overwhelmed with a desire to leave, to go anyplace but here, and find a life. She didn't have high expectations. *I just want a safe place to live where I am respected. Is that too much to ask? Just a little respect*, she said to herself. Jenna just decided to go on home.

———

On the kitchen counter was a note from Jenna's mother. "Your father and I will be out until midnight. Eat leftovers and clean up after yourself."

Jenna was pleased. She poured herself a glass of milk, grabbed a chicken leg, and sat down at the table. She ran to the phone and called Megan, her oldest and closest friend, and the only person she ever confided in about her parents.

"Megan," Jenna began. "Can you come over? Mother and Father are out tonight."

"I'll be right there. Do you want me to bring a movie or some games?"

"Can you bring your laptop?" asked Jenna.

"Sure can. I'll be right there," said Megan.

Jenna told Megan all about her discussion with the lady at the Circle of Hope. "The only way they'll help me is through a social services investigation and a court order."

"Your parents will beat you up just for talking to that lady," said Megan.

"Well, that's true, but I didn't tell them my name, and I made the call from the library, so they don't know who I am," said Jenna.

"That's good," said Megan. "I wish you could just come live with us."

"They don't even know I have a friend, and let's keep it that way," said Jenna, "so that when I disappear someday, they won't question you."

"So you're still planning to run away?" asked Megan.

"I comfort myself thinking about it all the time," said Jenna.

"Could you go live with some of your relatives?" asked Megan.

"Mom said I have no grandparents or aunts or uncles or cousins. I guess they're all dead," said Jenna. "Or maybe Mom was an only child.

"What about your dad's family?" asked Megan.

"I guess they're all gone too," answered Jenna.

"Would your mother tell you the truth about something like that?" asked Megan.

"She never told me the truth about anything," said Jenna.

"How could we find out?" asked Megan. "I brought my laptop."

"Maybe if I snoop through their things, I can figure out something," said Jenna. "Come on. I'm not allowed in their bedroom, so don't touch anything. Just sit on the floor and keep me company, while I snoop."

She looked through a shoebox that was full of pictures, old movie stubs, notes from girlfriends, and a church handout.

"That's odd," said Jenna. "I didn't know my mother ever went to church. Plain Community Christian Church; that could be any place in the United States."

Jenna opened another box, and this one had her mother's documents, such as her passport, her social security card, her birth certificate, and college transcripts. Jenna looked at her mother's birth certificate, and found out that her mother was born in Canton, Ohio.

"I'm writing down the names of my grandmother and grandfather. It's a place to start," said Jenna.

"Put everything away very carefully, exactly the way it was," said Megan.

Jenna turned off the light, and they went back downstairs. Jenna's heart was racing. "Let's look this stuff up on your laptop," said Jenna.

"Shhhh. I just heard something outside. I have a bad feeling," said Megan. "I'll go home and you call me when you can." Megan slipped out the back door, and seconds later, Jenna's parents burst in the front door.

Jenna hid the paper in her pocket that had her grandparents' names, and headed for her bedroom, but her mother called to her.

"Jenna. Stop right there," said her mother. "We just won a free trip to Rome, and we are leaving soon."

"Am I going too?" asked Jenna.

Her parents started laughing. "Now why would we take you?" asked Jenna's father. "Besides, there are only two tickets."

"Will I just stay here alone?" asked Jenna. "Just give me a little money and I'll be fine."

"We're not going to give you any money," said Jenna's father. "But we'll buy a little food for you, and you will stay here, for ten days, and not tell anyone you are home alone. You will go to school just like you always do."

Jenna picked up a paper weight from the desk, threw it on the floor, turned, and went up the stairs. *Ten days*, thought Jenna. *I would have been happy to have two days to get away. I just have to remember to keep acting angry.*

Chapter 2

Jenna decided that if she didn't have any living relatives in Ohio, she was going to buy a bus ticket for Miami, Florida, where it never gets very cold.

The next morning at school, Jenna found Megan right away. They shared a study hall, so they slipped into the library, and headed for the computers.

"My parents won a free vacation and they're leaving for Rome in one week!" said Jenna.

"They wouldn't leave you alone on Thanksgiving, would they?" asked Megan.

"They are going to, and it will be the most thankful Thanksgiving in my whole life," said Jenna.

"I guess this is the break you've been hoping for," said Megan. "Will you remember to call off school, so they don't call your mom?"

"Oh yes," said Jenna. "I will call the school, and in my best mommy voice, tell them that our daughter Jenna will be going to Rome with us."

"Will you write to me?" asked Megan.

"Yes, but don't you think I should make up a fake name, so your family won't suspect anything?" asked Jenna.

"How about Ashley Lorelle?" suggested Megan. "I met her at camp and she writes to me sometimes. My parents wouldn't suspect anything if I got letters from her."

"Good. Write it down for me," said Jenna. "I wouldn't want to spell her name wrong. Maybe I'll tell my grandparents that's my name, just in case they are as mean as Mom and Dad. Wait. Won't your parents notice if the postmark is from a different state than she's from?"

"I don't think they will notice, and if they do, I'll just tell them that she moved," said Megan. "Oh, I'm going to miss you so much." Megan wrote the name on a sticky note and handed it to Jenna, who hid it away in her purse. Megan got tears in her eyes, and Jenna picked up on it.

"I know we won't be neighbors anymore, but at least I won't be dead," said Jenna. "If I stick around here much longer, I will be."

"If this whole plan of yours backfires, I don't want to think about what might happen to you," said Megan.

"I have to do something," said Jenna. "My life is miserable. If I don't do this, I will never forgive myself."

"You're right," said Megan. "I do want the best for you. I'll try to be more supportive."

Jenna pulled her grandparents' names out of her purse. "Should we put their name in Google?" asked Jenna.

"No," answered Megan. "Let's try the white pages first.

"Why didn't I think of that?" asked Jenna as she typed the name Frederick Jones in Canton, Ohio, into the computer. Several names came up, but one had her grandmother's first name, Evelyn, listed with the household. "They're still alive," said Jenna. "Do you think they are really horrible people? They raised my mother, didn't they?"

"I bet they aren't as bad as your mother," said Megan. "Are you going to just show up on their doorstep?"

"Oh no," said Jenna. "I'm going to watch them. I might never tell them who I am. But it's a place to start."

"You're going to need money," said Megan. "My parents will give me money if I ask for something. Let me think."

"No," said Jenna. "My parents never give me a dime, but I have been planning this for a long time. They always leave plenty of money lying around. I take $5.00 sometimes and $10.00 other times. Sometimes, I just take a dollar. They never suspect a thing. I have over $450.00 hidden in my room. I will buy a ticket and hop on a bus.

When I get there, I will look for a cheap hotel. If they ask me where my parents are, I will tell them that I am 22 or something. People can't really tell how old we are."

"Are you taking everything you own?" asked Megan.

"Well, I don't have that much, but no, I'm barely taking anything," said Jenna. "After that ice storm last week, I'm taking a heavy winter coat. It's one of my mother's, but she hasn't worn it in years."

"Don't you have sentimental things to take, like CD's, pictures, or clothes?" asked Megan.

"I want them to think I was kidnapped, or had an accident, or possibly got scared and went to stay with a friend, so I'm not taking anything but an old purse and my mom's old coat," said Jenna.

"Good idea," said Megan. "They probably won't call the police, because they would have to admit that they left you alone."

"That's what I'm counting on," said Jenna. "Eventually, they will probably hire someone to look for me. That is why I don't want it to look like I ran away. And if they ask you any questions, tell them that I was a real snob and never talked to you."

"That won't work," said Megan. "People at school see us together."

"Don't worry about it. They won't let a private detective talk to the school," said Jenna.

"You will say 'good-bye' to me won't you?" asked Megan.

"I promise. The moment my parents leave, I will say 'good-bye' to you, and then head for the bus station."

Chapter 3

Jenna walked quickly to the bus station. She was extremely self-conscious carrying the heavy, out-of-style winter coat, since it was fifty-five degrees outside, unseasonably warm for November, even in New Jersey. She bought a ticket for Canton, Ohio, and then sat waiting for just ten minutes. Thankful that no one she knew was getting on, Jenna boarded the bus and sat by an elderly lady, who was taking a nap.

As the bus departed, Jenna smiled as she looked through the small, overnight bag that Megan had bought her. It contained a cute nightgown, bathroom supplies, slippers, and a little no-contract cell phone with three hundred minutes on it. Megan had put her cell phone number in it, and made Jenna promise to call her every Sunday night. Under the nightgown, Jenna found a stylish wallet with a school picture of Megan. She also had two twenty-dollar bills and a note that said "emergency money." Megan was so thoughtful and Jenna wondered if she would ever find a good friend like that in Ohio.

Jenna leaned back and closed her eyes. She felt different and realized that the void feeling in her chest was gone. It was filled with something new. *It was hope. Oh, I hope that my grandmother will like me and not make me go back. And I hope that my grandfather won't let anything bad happen to me.*

In Canton, Ohio, Jenna had an aunt named Cheryl Workman, who she never heard of. Cheryl Workman taught Special Education. A new student named Eric had been placed in a foster home and as a result, was in Cheryl's reading class. On Friday morning, the class was reviewing literature terms. Eric interrupted the lesson several times and the other students were just as annoyed as Cheryl was. Finally Shane had to say something.

"Why do you have to talk all the time?" Shane asked.

"I don't," said Eric.

"Yes, you do," added Scottie, "and it's really annoying."

"Well sorry I'm so annoying," yelled Eric. He went out of the room and slammed the door.

"Can he just leave the room like that?" asked David.

"It's in his IEP that he can leave the room anytime he needs to unwind," said Cheryl.

"I heard that Eric completely blew up at his last foster home, and tore up the place," said Scottie. "He's crazy."

"Well we don't know what kind of things he's been through," said Cheryl. "Maybe he was abused."

"That is no excuse," said David. "I remember things that happened to me when I was little, before I got adopted. But I'm not going to freak out on my Mom and Dad."

"That's because you got a wonderful family that would do anything for you," said Cheryl. "Eric has been bounced around from one foster home to another."

"Maybe if he would behave himself, someone would keep him," said Hailey.

"I agree with David. There is no excuse to behave like a jerk," said Shane. "I'm not even allowed to see my mom. I could just start punching through walls. Sometimes I feel like it, but I don't do it. It wouldn't do any good."

"I'm sure you two are the exceptions," said Cheryl. "Most kids act out when they have had bad things happen to them."

"What about me?" Hailey asked. "The last three years I lived with my dad and we were buds. Now he has a new wife. She doesn't like me, so I have to live with my mom now, and I hate it. You don't see me storming out of the room."

"You all do behave pretty well most of the time. Well except for Scottie. You get in trouble a lot," said Cheryl.

"That's true," said Scottie, "but it's usually just for socializing."

"You're probably right," said Cheryl. "But if it weren't for the things you guys have been through, you wouldn't even be in my class."

"What do you mean?" asked Shane.

"You four all know that you're smart," said Cheryl. "You wouldn't be in special education classes at all if you wouldn't have had some trauma in your life. There was a time when you couldn't focus on school work and you got behind. So they gave you an IEP and you were placed in these classes."

All four students were quiet for a while. Cheryl erased the board and got ready for her next class.

Finally Shane said, "You're saying that we don't even belong in special education?"

"I'm saying that many kids in special education are here because something went wrong in their life," said Cheryl. "My nephew was doing just fine in school. But he broke his leg and missed a lot of school, and he never caught up with his classmates. After a while, they had him tested and put him in special education. Even though you guys didn't break any bones, you know there was a time in your life when you couldn't concentrate at school. Maybe you still can't concentrate sometimes."

Later that evening, Cheryl was home with her family. It was getting dark, and Susan, Cheryl's daughter, had to go out to the shed to get the step-ladder for her mother, who wanted to begin putting up Christmas lights in the house. It was only November 20th, but her mother always finished decorating before Thanksgiving. Susan opened the shed door, lifted the ladder off the hook, and turned to leave. Then she heard a floorboard creak in the back of the shed. She caught her breath, looked back into the darkness, and thought she saw a dark figure. Trembling, she ran for the house.

"Mom. Dad. There's someone in the shed," shouted Susan.

Inside the shed, shivering from head to toe, was Jenna. She had watched the house next door for a long time, and when no one came outside, she decided to warm up in a neighbor's shed. *Oh no*, thought Jenna. *What am I going to do now? I should get out of here- and fast.*

Richie Workman came charging out the door with a pellet gun, and he went right to the shed.

"Come on out of there!" shouted Richie.

"Don't hurt me," said Jenna, as she emerged from the shed. "I didn't take anything. My feet just got cold, so I went inside to try and warm up."

Richie regarded the girl for a moment and finally said, "I guess you'd better come inside. You look pretty harmless to me."

Jenna felt very self-conscious as she entered the kitchen. Her eyes were tearing up, and her mother's old-fashioned coat felt way too big for her. Her feet were completely numb in her little tennis shoes. She hugged her overnight bag, trying to get a shred of courage. A family stood staring at her.

"This is our prowler," said Richie. "Should we call the cops?"

Jenna looked at them and the tears finally rolled down her cheeks.

"Oh don't cry, we're not going to call the cops," said Cheryl. "My name is Cheryl Workman, and this is my husband Richie. Right here is Susan and over there, hiding behind the sofa, are the twins, Drew and Will. We have two more boys, but they are out."

"I'm glad to meet you," said Jenna. "Thank you so much for not calling the cops."

"You look kind of familiar," said Cheryl. "Do you go to our church? Do you go to Susan's school?"

"No," answered Jenna. "I'm really not from around here. I'm just passing through."

"What's your name?" asked Richie.

Jenna froze. *What was the name of Megan's friend?* Jenna could feel the paper in her pocket, where she put it while she was on the bus, but she couldn't pull it out and read it now.

"My name is Jenna Ashcraft," said Jenna. She thought that honesty was the best policy until she saw the shocked look on Cheryl's face.

"Where are you from, Jenna?" asked Cheryl.

"If you don't mind, I would rather not say," said Jenna. Jenna had a very bad feeling and suddenly wanted to head for the Budget Hotel a few streets away. She moved toward the back door where she came in.

"Are you Cynthia's girl?" asked Cheryl.

Jenna couldn't believe her ears. Just hearing her mother's name sent shivers through her already frozen body.

Richie was really puzzled and asked, "You mean your sister Cynthia?"

Jenna studied Cheryl's face and realized that she looked a lot like her mother, only not so severe.

"Now I know why she looks familiar," said Cheryl. "She looks like Susan."

"Did something happen to your parents?" asked Susan. "Is that why you came to see us?"

"I was actually looking for Frederick and Evelyn Jones," said Jenna. "I just wanted to peek at them and see what they're like."

"Do your parents know you're here?" asked Cheryl.

"Oh, please don't tell them," said Jenna. "I will go away and not cause any trouble."

"Did you run away?" asked Richie.

"Not exactly," said Jenna. "They went on vacation, so they don't even know I'm gone. There is a motel down the street and I'm just going to go there now."

"Harold and Cynthia went on vacation and left you alone at Thanksgiving time," said Cheryl. "Well they haven't changed one bit."

Jenna started crying and she didn't know why. Cheryl walked across the room and put her arms around her. Jenna couldn't remember getting hugged like that before.

"I didn't even know that Mother had a sister," said Jenna.

"We have a brother too, and he has three kids," said Cheryl. "Your father has two brothers, but they don't have any children. Harold's parents only have one grandchild and it's you. My mother tells me that they are heartbroken that they don't get to see their only granddaughter."

"Mother and Father told me that my grandparents were dead. I looked through Mother's things and found her birth certificate. Then I searched the internet and found my grandparents' address. As soon as my parents left for Rome, I hopped on a bus and came here. If my grandparents are as mean as Mother and Father, I'm going to some big city and just disappear."

"They aren't mean at all," said Cheryl. "My mother cries every night because she lost Cynthia. She blames herself for spoiling her, but Cynthia was the most selfish person I ever met. She married Harold and told my parents that she never wanted to hear from them again. We wouldn't even know about you, but Harold's parents somehow found out that they had a baby girl named Jenna, and told us. Harold and Cynthia don't talk to Harold's parents either."

"Don't you think we should tell Grandma and Grandpa that she's here?" asked Susan.

"I don't want to give them a heart attack," said Cheryl. "Maybe we should tell them tomorrow."

"They're just watching TV," said Susan. "What if I went over and told them that we have a visitor and we are bringing her over to meet them?"

Richie and Cheryl looked out the window. Evelyn saw them looking and went over and opened the window. Cheryl opened the kitchen window.

"I saw you guys looking at us," said Evelyn. "Is something wrong?"

"No Mom," said Cheryl. "Actually, something wonderful has happened. Can we come over for a few minutes?"

"Of course Dear," said Evelyn.

"Boys, maybe you should stay here. Go up and get ready for bed," said Cheryl. "We're going to Grandma and Grandpa's."

Everybody just walked out the door, across the driveway, and into Fred and Evelyn's house. Jenna felt like she stood out as she entered the room, with her giant coat and tiny wet tennis shoes.

"Mom, Dad, you won't believe who this is," said Cheryl, as she put her arm around Jenna and brought her forward into the room. "This is Jenna, Cynthia's daughter."

Evelyn put her hand over her mouth and stood still, looking shocked. Jenna was afraid that her grandmother was upset to see her.

"Can this be true?" asked Evelyn.

"Jenna found Cynthia's birth certificate and looked you up on the internet," said Richie. "She came to Canton all by herself, just to get a look at her grandparents. She didn't even know she had aunts and uncles and cousins."

"I can't believe Cynthia would let her go," said Fred.

"They went to Rome and left her home alone," said Susan.

"Well, that I believe," said Fred.

"They don't even know she's here." said Susan.

"Are you planning to just go back home and not tell them you came here?" asked Fred.

"No," answered Jenna. "I'm never going back there. I would rather go to jail. I was thinking about going to a city like Miami, and just become another run-away teen."

"How old are you Jenna?" asked Susan.

"I'm seventeen," answered Jenna. "My birthday was two weeks ago. They never even mentioned it."

"I'm seventeen too!" said Susan.

"I don't think so," said Cheryl.

"I'm not seventeen?" asked Susan.

"I don't think Jenna is seventeen," said Cheryl. "Mother, do you remember how you cried for days when Harold's mother called and said that Cynthia had a baby girl named Jenna, and that we were never going to see her? Well, I was expecting Susan at the time. In fact, I just found out. I went ahead and told you that I was expecting again, so you would stop crying."

"You think I'm eighteen," said Jenna. "Why would they lie about that?"

"Why would they tell you that your grandparents were dead?" asked Fred.

"They lie about everything," said Jenna, "but sooner or later I was going to need my birth certificate. That's probably why they make me drive at night, without a license."

"Don't you see, Sweetie?" said Cheryl. "If you are eighteen, you can live with us, and there is nothing they can do about it. You are an adult, and you can live where you want."

"How will I prove that I'm eighteen?" asked Jenna.

"You live somewhere in New Jersey, don't you?" asked Fred. "With your help, we can track down your birth certificate. We'll make some calls in the morning."

"Mom, can Jenna sleep in my room?" asked Susan.

"Maybe she can sleep in Cynthia's room," said Evelyn. Jenna looked so scared that Evelyn had to ask, "Do they mistreat you Jenna?"

Jenna looked down at the floor.

"Don't you worry about a thing, Honey," said Fred. "You are here now, and everything's going to be OK."

"Can I hug my granddaughter?" asked Evelyn gently, looking at Jenna.

Jenna went into her arms, and once again was amazed at the hug.

"It's getting late," said Fred. "Where do you want to spend the night?"

"Well, I'm not ready to see my mother's room, just yet, so could I sleep in Susan's room, since she offered?" asked Jenna.

"Do you have a suitcase?" asked Cheryl.

"No. I didn't bring anything but this overnight bag, and the clothes I'm wearing," said Jenna. "I want them to think I got kidnapped."

Jenna looked back at her grandparents and smiled, as she was whisked away to the house next door. When they went into the kitchen, the other two boys, Shawn and Josh, were raiding the cupboards and the refrigerator.

"I wondered where you guys went," said Shawn. "I thought you were going to stay home and decorate for Christmas."

"Well look what we found out in the shed," said Susan. "It's our cousin Jenna."

"Do we have a cousin Jenna?" asked Josh.

"You know about Mom's sister named Cynthia, who never speaks to her. She lives in New Jersey, and is married to a man named Harold," said Susan. "This is their daughter Jenna, and she ran away."

"She looks just like you," Josh said to Susan.

"That's funny," said Susan to Josh, "because I think Jenna looks exactly like you."

"Well her hair looks like yours," said Josh.

"Are you guys in high school?" asked Jenna.

"I'm a senior," said Josh, "and Shawn goes to Kent branch. We both work at the mall. What about you Jenna?"

"I'm a junior, but your mom thinks I'm already eighteen. Now why would my parents lie to me about my age?" asked Jenna.

"Maybe they weren't ready to send you to kindergarten when the time came," said Susan.

"Well, that's hard to believe," said Jenna. "They probably couldn't wait for me to go to school. It's more likely that they forgot how old I was."

Jenna was so hungry, and the boys just kept handing her food to eat; leftover pizza, pasta salad, chips, and juice. Food never tasted so good before. *Could life really be this wonderful?* Jenna thought.

"Are you finished eating?" asked Susan. "If you are, let's go up to my room and find you something to sleep in."

"Oh, I have a nightgown," said Jenna. "My best friend got me a few things before I left. We thought it would be smart if all my clothes were still there. I wonder if they will even report that I'm missing."

Susan gave Jenna her sofa to sleep on and all kinds of clothes that she didn't want anymore.

"You know," said Susan. "Shawn and Josh have each other, and Drew and Will have each other. I always thought I was missing someone. Now I know that it was you. I hope they can't take you away from us."

"I hope I really am eighteen," said Jenna, "and they won't be able to do anything. But I don't want to be a burden to your family."

"You won't be a burden," said Susan.

Chapter 4

Saturday went by very quickly as the family decorated both houses inside and out. Jenna was overwhelmed by the twinkling lights, the cozy aromas of cinnamon and pine, and the sound of Christmas carols. Jenna's parents' idea of preparing for the holidays was stocking up on liquor.

Grandpa Fred did not help decorate because he spent hours at his computer trying to locate Jenna's birth certificate. Once he located it online, he was able to fill out a form, pay with his credit card, and have it sent to his home. The man on the phone confirmed Cheryl's belief that Jenna was eighteen years old, so the family felt relieved that Harold and Cynthia could not bring any charges against them or against Jenna. To celebrate, they planned a big party for Sunday after church, with relatives coming from both sides of Jenna's family. Jenna was told that Harold's mother could not stop crying, and that she was cooking all day to bring her favorite dishes for her little granddaughter, who she thought she would never get to see.

That evening Jenna and Susan sat in Susan's room, talking like old friends.

"What are you doing Jenna?" asked Susan.

"I'm pinching myself," said Jenna. "I never thought it was possible to have a nice family, not to mention a family with a girl cousin my age, two cute little twin boy cousins, and two cool guy cousins who like feeding me snacks. And I love Grandmother and Grandfather."

"Grandma and Grandpa," said Susan.

"That's right," said Jenna. "And your mom and dad are super nice."

"Just wait until you meet Uncle Jack," said Susan. "He's so much fun. And he has a wife, Karen, and three little girls."

"Will they be there tomorrow?" asked Jenna.

"No," said Susan. "He's a preacher, so they can't get away on such short notice. They live in Cincinnati, but they are coming for Thanksgiving. You will meet them soon."

Sunday morning was very interesting to Jenna, because she had never been to church before. The music was very pretty, but Jenna didn't try to sing along. And she didn't bow her head during the prayers, even though the thought did occur to her, that if there was a god, maybe he had something to do with her finding her family. The sermon was on gratefulness, since it was just days before Thanksgiving. *If I had to go back today, to my miserable home, I would be grateful the rest of my life for this weekend,* thought Jenna.

Jenna's relatives lavished their love on her, and she treasured every moment. The hardest part of the day was when the two grandmothers sat Jenna down, and wanted some news about Harold and Cynthia.

"Well, let me think," said Jenna. "They are pretty successful in their careers. My father is a lawyer and my mother is the mayor in our city. They have a lot of friends." Then there was an awkward silence.

"What are you good at Dear?" asked Harold's mother. "Do you play sports, or music, or are you good at art?"

"I, ah, am pretty good at math," said Jenna.

Harold's father was listening, and he burst out with his thoughts. "What do you think, Helen? Do you think they took her to soccer practice and piano lessons? I bet those two scoundrels didn't spend one penny on the girl, except to buy her the necessities. I wouldn't be surprised if she was terribly neglected."

Everyone in the house stared at Jenna, waiting for a response. Finally, she decided to just tell the truth. "It was worse than neglect, although I never did without food. Well, not very often. It was close to abuse, and many times, I was struck by one or both of them. They screamed at me all the time. They hate me, and I have no idea why." Jenna could hear family members all over the room, as they caught their breath in shock.

"Well, we have no idea why they hate us either," said Harold's mother, "but from now on, you are with all of us. OK Honey?"

"For so long," said Jenna, "all I hoped for was just a little respect and a little peace. I never dreamed that I might have a loving, caring family someplace. They told me my grandparents were dead. I never even considered that I might have aunts and uncles and cousins. If you all want me, I want to stay very much."

Harold's mother started crying. "You know, Jenna. For years, I've had an empty spot in my heart. Every time my friends talk about their grandchildren, or say they are babysitting, or post pictures of them, I feel so jealous, and then I get angry with myself that I'm jealous. Oh please don't leave us."

Jenna went and sat by her Grandma Helen, and held her hand. And the tears ran down her cheeks again. Jenna hadn't cried since she was a tiny girl, and now she can't stop.

"Will you call me Grammy, Dear?" asked Helen. "I always wanted to have a grandchild and be called Grammy." Jenna squeezed her hand gently, and nodded her head.

"I guess you can call me Papa John," said her Grandfather Ashcraft, who sat down on the other side of Jenna.

"Jenna," said her Grandma Evelyn. "Fred and I have eight other beautiful grandchildren, but that doesn't mean we haven't missed you. All these years we go back and forth between feeling so angry with Harold and Cynthia that our health suffers or feeling depressed and injured that our children could treat us this way, keeping us away from our own grandchild. It has been like you were dead. So you see, we have suffered too."

"I always thought that I was the only victim of my parents' selfishness, but now I realize that there are others," said Jenna. Jenna hugged and kissed her wonderful relatives, and went home with Richie, Cheryl, and her cousins.

"Jenna, will you be OK tomorrow when we go to school?" asked Cheryl.

"You're all going to be gone tomorrow?" asked Jenna.

"Richie has a hardware store and works there, and the rest of us go to one school or another," said Cheryl. "I teach at the middle school. We have to go three days until Thanksgiving."

"Mom, should I pick up some papers in the office to enroll Jenna at my high school?" asked Susan.

"Good idea," said Cheryl. "Jenna, can you write out the name and address of your high school for Susan, so that our high school can send for your records?"

Jenna looked very worried and said, "Oh no, then Mother and Father will know where I am."

"I talked to my parents about it," said Cheryl. "The sooner we let Harold and Cynthia know where you are, the better. That way, they can't accuse us of doing anything wrong."

"No, please don't tell them. Please," begged Jenna. "At least don't tell them until they come home from Rome. Just give me those seven days. I need those last seven days when they don't know I'm missing."

"Ok, Jenna, just relax," said Cheryl. "Next Monday, a week from today, Thanksgiving will be over and your parents will be home. When I get home from school that day, I will call your parents and tell them that you are here, that you are eighteen, and that you plan to stay with us."

Deep down, Jenna knew it would be better when things were settled with her parents, but right now, she didn't want to think about them. This was Jenna's third night to sleep in Susan's room, and she was so happy she could burst.

Since it was Sunday night, Jenna went into the bedroom and got her cell phone and called Megan, her neighbor girl back home, and let her know all that had happened. Megan was very happy for Jenna, especially that Jenna was eighteen years old, and should not be in trouble with the law for running away.

"Jenna," asked Megan, "would it be alright if I tell my mom and dad about all of this? I've been really uncomfortable keeping secrets from them."

"You can, but please ask them not to tell anyone about me until after Thanksgiving vacation. My aunt is going to break the news to them as soon as they get home from Rome," said Jenna.

"I'll let them know," said Megan. "Have a very happy Thanksgiving. I know I will now that I know you're safe!"

"Oh, and thank you so much for my nightgown and my overnight bag and everything you gave me. I was so scared that day, and those things were such a comfort to me," said Jenna. "I'll call you next Sunday night."

Chapter 5

Early Monday morning, Cheryl got a call from her friend Kinsey. "Start doing your snow dance! Did you hear the weather reports? There's a snowstorm on the way."

"Are you serious?" asked Cheryl. "We didn't listen to the news all weekend."

"Actually, they didn't say much about it last night. But the storm has expanded and is heading right toward us," said Kinsey.

As the family ate a pancake breakfast, prepared by Jenna, they listened to the TV weather reports. Snow was falling in areas to the west. A list of school closings were scrolling across the bottom of the screen, but their school was not among them.

"Jenna, did you see that forecast for snow?" asked Cheryl. "Don't go anyplace unless it's next door to see your grandparents."

"We should have a snow day!" yelled Drew. "What are they waiting for?"

"They never call a snow day until we actually get some snow," said Cheryl. "It might just fizzle out. Now you kids hurry up and get your coats on, and today you need to wear your boots, gloves, and those hats with face masks. We don't know what it will be like later when we come home."

Will and Drew put on so many clothes that they looked like Eskimos.

"How do I look Mom?" asked Will.

"Like you are ready for anything," said Cheryl.

"I am," said Will. "I'm ready to build the biggest fort ever."

Richie came in just then and said, "Cheryl, I was just watching the news, and the storm that was headed for Michigan is gigantic and is now spreading into Ohio, Indiana, Kentucky, and many other states. The temperature is dropping rapidly. We're in for a blizzard."

"Well, they haven't called a snow day yet," said Cheryl, "so I have to go to work."

"A couple of the local schools just called off," said Richie. "Maybe yours will too."

Just then the school bus pulled up and Drew and Will ran and got on. Richie took off for work in one car and Shawn left for an early class in his old truck. Cheryl took Josh and Susan to drop off at the high school, before heading for her teaching job at the middle school.

Jenna was left alone for the first time since she ran away from home. She ran to the window and saw thick clouds rolling in. *I had better get in the shower fast,* she thought. *I don't want to be in my night clothes if that storm comes this way.*

It started snowing about the time the elementary students arrived at school. After about a half hour, there was heavy snowfall with limited visibility. The kids were very excited, but the teachers looked nervously out the windows, worrying about the drive home.

Around 10 a.m., the principal passed the word around that the busses were pulling up at the elementary schools to take the little ones home first. He said to tell only the adults, because it could take a while before the busses arrive at the middle and high schools. Cheryl heard the news from the teacher next door, Kinsey, who was also one of her best friends. Kinsey saw the shocked look on Cheryl's face.

"I'm sure your boys will be fine Cheryl," said Kinsey. "The bus driver won't leave them until they get inside the house, and didn't you say that your niece is there?"

"Yes, Jenna is there, and my parents are next door, and Shawn promised to come home after his class," Cheryl said. She looked back into her room. Her students were out of their seats, looking out the windows.

"Mrs. Workman," said Cheyanne, "Look at the snow on those benches outside."

"Yes," Cheryl answered. "It's really deep. Have you seen any snow plows go by?"

"Are you kidding? We can't even see the road." said Adam. "Do you think we'll get home safely?"

"I must admit that I'm getting worried about that," said Cheryl.

Cheryl ran to the phone in her room and quickly called her home number. She got a busy signal. *We have call waiting, so what does that mean?*

Just then the classroom phone rang. Cheryl grabbed it, hoping it was a call from home.

"Send Eddie and Melissa to the office," said the secretary. "Eddie's mom is here to take them home." Cheryl sent them out, and ran to the window to look out again. If anything, it was even worse outside. She wondered if the two kids would even get home.

Cheryl heard static and the principal came on the loud speaker. "The police have declared that nothing is allowed on the roads except snow plows and emergency vehicles," he said. "That means we will all be spending the night right here in the middle school. In the building next door, the high school students are being told the same thing. It is extremely important that none of you leave the building. This storm is very dangerous. Your parents will be very relieved to know that you will all be safe for tonight, and we will be sending out a call to them very soon. We will follow our normal schedule, and then at the end of the school day, everyone will return to your first period class, which will be your home for the night. In between classes you are free to use your cell phones to reassure family members. The good news is that there is plenty of food in the cafeteria and our cooks are all stuck here with us."

The bell rang and the students all went to their next class. Cheryl took the opportunity to call home again. Once again, it rang busy. She ran down the hall to the office, and found Eddie's mom crying in there, because the policeman wouldn't let her take the kids and leave. Cheryl took her aside to ask her a question.

"Mrs. Johnson, my boys were sent home on a bus from the elementary. I've been trying to call them. Have you seen any busses out there?

"They were all over the place," said Eddie's mom. "That's why I wanted to get the kids home myself. And now I'm stuck here too and I just want to go home. I don't do well with kids this age, unless they're my own."

"I have Eddie in my first period class, so he will be with me all night. Would you like to join us? It's a pretty nice class, and I would enjoy having some adult company," Cheryl said.

"I haven't given up on taking off, but if I'm stuck here, I would like to join you. Thanks for offering," said Eddie's mom.

Marilyn, the secretary overheard their conversation. "Cheryl, you go on back to your class and I will call the bus garage and find out where your boys are."

"Why didn't I think of that?" asked Cheryl. "What would I do without you?"

The bus garage was in total chaos. The phone rang constantly, and no one was free to answer it. Every single bus was still out on the road; some were stuck in drifts and others were slowly dropping off elementary students. The wind was blowing heavy snow, making it impossible to see more than a few feet away.

Angie Knight had been driving a bus for twenty-two years and had never seen anything like this. Today was her worst nightmare. She had only dropped off four children, and she had another twenty-six to go. The snow was so high that the bus could barely move down the road. At last she reached the home of Drew and Will Workman, and unfortunately, they had a long driveway. The visibility was so bad and the temperature was so low, that Angie knew she had to walk the children to the door herself.

"Children, I'm going to walk Drew and Will to their door," Angie said. "It is very dangerous outside. Now you stay in your seats until I get back." She took each boy by the hand and headed up the driveway.

"This way Miss Knight," said Will. "We can go in through the garage." Angie wondered how he could even see the garage. The snow was up to Angie's knees and up to the boys' thighs. Finally they reached the garage door. Drew stood on his toes and punched in the code. The garage door went up and they ran over and opened the door to the house. Jenna met them at the door.

"Oh, I'm so glad someone is home for the boys," said Angie. "The weather outside is life-threatening. I still have twenty-four students to drop off and my bus can barely travel through this snow. The next ten stops are out in the boonies, and I'm afraid we will get stuck out there and we will all die."

"Why don't you bring them in here?" suggested Jenna. "That way you will all be safe."

"You know, that is a very good idea," said Angie. "I'll go get the kids."

Jenna suddenly realized what she did. She just invited twenty-five people into a house that was not her own. She was wondering what kind of trouble she will be in. She tried to watch Angie go down the driveway, but she couldn't see anything but blowing snow.

Angie felt bad about leaving the bus in the middle of the road, so she backed the bus carefully and then turned into the Workman's driveway. She was so thankful that she was still able to move the bus. Angie told the children that they were to hold hands and that their lives depended on getting to Will and Drew's garage safely.

Back in the house, Drew said to Jenna, "Those little kindergarten kids can't walk through that snow. Look how high it came on me."

"Maybe I should go help," said Jenna.

"You should," said Will. "Drew, let's go hide our best toys. Junior Smith will tear them to pieces when he gets in here."

"You're right," said Drew. "We should hide everything."

Jenna didn't have any boots of her own, but she saw a pair of sturdy-looking boots next to the garage door and she put them on. Then she put on someone's heavy coat, gloves, and scarf that were hanging on the hook. She walked through the garage and trudged through the deep foot-steps of the bus driver, finally reaching the bus door.

"Oh thank goodness you came to help," said Angie. "We have to carry the little ones."

"I can do that," said Jenna. Angie sent Jenna through the snow with two of the bigger girls.

"Come on up to the front seats, kids. I'm going to call the bus garage while we wait for that big girl to get back," Angie said. It took her a while to get through to the bus garage. Finally she got hold of Ray, who was in charge of bussing. She explained what they were doing.

"Good job Angie. Call me from the house when you have them all in and we will notify the parents," said Ray. "Of all the bus drivers out there, you are in the best state right now. Please pray for the others. This is a very grave situation."

"Thanks Ray," said Angie. "I'll let you know first thing when we get them all in." Angie thought she was going to cry, but she knew the kids would get more scared if she did. She clenched her teeth and pretended to look out the frosty window. Then she walked through the bus, bringing lunch boxes and backpacks to the front. She checked under each seat, making sure there weren't any stragglers. After what seemed like hours, Jenna stepped up on the bus.

"I hope you don't mind, but I took a few minutes and got the kids blankets and made them sit down and watch a movie," said Jenna. "I just don't want them running through the house getting into trouble."

"You did a good thing," said Angie. "We just need to get the rest of them inside."

Then they stepped off the bus, with Jenna carrying two children and Angie one. The snow was even deeper and the wind even stronger. They made many trips to the house and back.

"How are you doing Angie?" screamed Jenna. The wind and snow were overwhelming.

Angie didn't have the breath or the energy to answer, but she reached a hand out and patted Jenna's shoulder, so she knew she was still there. This final trip took longer than all of the others. Angie couldn't feel her legs, but somehow they still moved through the deep trench created by their bodies moving through the snow.

As Angie took the last child into the house, Jenna asked, "Angie, do you think I should close the garage door?" Before Angie could answer, a person came into the garage, completely covered with snow.

"It's me, Shawn," he shouted. "Let's leave the door open, in case Dad gets home somehow."

"How did you ever get here?" asked Jenna, as they brushed the snow off their clothes and went into the house.

"My truck got stuck in the parking lot at school and so I decided to just walk home. The hardest part was figuring out where I was all the time. What on earth is all this?" Shawn asked, as he came into the family room and saw little people everywhere.

"Well, the bus couldn't really go any farther, so Angie, the bus driver, and I brought them all in here," said Jenna. "I hope I'm not in trouble with your family."

"If you want to invite thirty or forty children into the house, you're probably welcome to do that," said Shawn.

"There aren't thirty or forty," said Jenna. She looked around and found Angie in the kitchen, just hanging up the phone.

"Ray, at the bus garage, is so relieved that we're all safe. Someone is going to call all of their parents," said Angie. "Did you know that your phone was off the hook and beeping? Someone might have tried to call you."

"You know, she's right," said Shawn. "I tried to call. I'm going to call Mom's cell phone, and tell her I'm alright. Are Drew and Will here?"

"Yes, they're here someplace," said Jenna.

"What about Susan and Josh?" asked Shawn.

"I haven't seen them," said Jenna.

Chapter 6

Shawn called his mother, who was very relieved that they were safely home. She explained to Shawn that she, Josh, and Susan would be spending the night at the school, and that their dad was stuck at his work for the night.

"Uh Mom, I think Jenna has something important to tell you," Shawn said, handing Jenna the phone with a smirk on his face.

Jenna looked surprised, but took the phone. "Hi. When Drew and Will arrived, the bus driver said the bus could barely go through the deep snow and she was afraid they were all going to die," said Jenna.

"So?" asked Cheryl.

"So we brought the children in here. There are twenty-four of them here, plus the bus driver," said Jenna. "I hope you're not mad at me."

"Of course not," said Cheryl, "but you're going to have to take care of them and feed them."

"I was just going to start making hot chocolate and popcorn," said Jenna.

"That's good," said Cheryl. "And for dinner, there are four packages of hot dogs in the freezer and enough buns. And look in the pantry for cans of vegetables and fruits. Make sure they all get plenty to eat. Get Shawn to help you."

"Aunt Cheryl. Thanks for not being mad," said Jenna.

"You might have saved a bunch of lives," said Cheryl. "Now take good care of those kids."

Jenna hung up the phone and looked at Shawn. "Did you say that your dad isn't coming home?"

"Yes," answered Shawn. "He's stuck at work. I'll go close the garage door, since no one else is coming."

Then the phone started ringing. The worried parents wanted to talk to their children. Jenna let Angie handle the phone calls as she and Shawn made bag after bag of popcorn and tons of hot chocolate.

Cheryl was very relieved that her family members were all safe and not out in the storm. As the kids changed classes, she stepped out into the hall and visited with Kinsey next door.

"Kinsey, have you heard from your family yet?" asked Cheryl.

"Yes and no," said Kinsey. "Ken is fine and the kids are staying in their dorms all day, so they're fine. But my parents had doctor appointments today, and I'm afraid they might be out on the road some place. They aren't answering their phones."

"Maybe they just don't have a signal," said Cheryl.

Just then Lesley came down the hall with tears in her eyes. "Marilyn called the bus garage to check on Zoe and Zack for me. Their bus didn't make it to our house. She thinks it's stuck someplace," she said. "They're all going to freeze to death." The three of them looked out the classroom windows. They couldn't see anything but white.

Ray from the bus garage called the house and asked for Angie. Ray praised Angie for getting all of the kids into the house and told her that he had all of the other bus drivers take the children into the house where they were. He reached all of the busses except for one. Then he asked Angie if she saw any other busses and she told him that she had not. He explained that Bus 12 that Phyllis drives did not return to the garage and she had not checked in or answered Ray for a long time. After she hung up, Angie told Shawn and Jenna about the phone call.

"I saw a bus," said Shawn.

"Where," asked Angie.

"Well it wasn't very far from here," said Shawn. "I walked right by it when I walked home. It was Bus 12 too; I remember because that was my bus number for years."

"Was it moving?" asked Angie.

"Well, not when I went by it, but it could have moved after that," said Shawn.

"That's not likely," said Angie. "You came in when we were all finished moving the kids into the house, and that was about an hour after I gave up moving my bus through the snow. Did you notice anyone on the bus, by the way?"

"No," answered Shawn. "But the storm was so loud, I couldn't hear anything else."

Angie called Ray and told him what Shawn said about Bus 12.

"Angie," said Ray. "Bus 12 is out there some place with between twenty-two and twenty-eight children and a bus driver. And Phyllis isn't answering when I call. Emergency vehicles are not moving any better than school busses. There is no one out there looking for them and these parents are out of their minds with worry. If we don't rescue those kids soon, their parents will go out on the roads."

Angie hung up and looked over at Shawn.

"No!" Shawn said.

"No, I wouldn't want you to go out there," said Angie. "I was just looking at you for ideas."

"I'm very lucky that I made it home alive," said Shawn. "All the way home I kept thinking how mad Mom would be at me if I lost my way or if I froze to death or if I got frost bite. I'm not going back out there."

"Even if he did go out there, and he found a bunch of kids, he couldn't get them back here alone," said Jenna. "We barely made it, and I'm sure the snow is even deeper now than it was then."

"I know," said Angie. "And I need you both to help me take care of these kids."

The three of them just stood there, thinking about how they couldn't do anything to help those kids on the bus. Suddenly they heard a huge gust of wind that shook the house. The power went off and the children all screamed. Then the power came back on.

"We could soon lose the power for good," said Angie. "Do you have any candles, flashlights, or battery lamps?"

"I don't know where they keep anything," said Jenna. "Do you know where those things are Shawn?"

"What?" Shawn asked. He looked very distracted.

"Do you know where they keep the candles and flashlights?" asked Jenna.

Shawn walked over to a drawer and pulled out a flashlight. He handed it to Angie. "I don't know where they keep the candles," he said. Then he walked across the room, opened the door, and went into the garage.

Jenna followed him and opened the door. "Where are you going?" she asked.

"I'm looking for something," Shawn said. He walked around, opening boxes and looking on shelves. Finally he grabbed a huge box and came back in the house.

"What's in that box?" asked Jenna.

"It's a rope," said Shawn. "We made it in youth group. It's around 150 yards long, the length of one and a half football fields, and about the length of Noah's Ark."

"What are you going to do with that," asked Angie.

"I was thinking that I could go out with the rope," said Shawn. "Jenna, you could stay in the garage and unwind the rope, and if I don't reach the bus by the time I'm out of rope, I will just come back home."

"What if you reach the bus?" asked Angie. "You won't be able to bring twenty-two children here."

"We could at least report where they are and what condition they are in."

"Wear your warmest clothes," said Jenna. "And maybe two pair of socks and a hat and a hood."

"I actually have electric socks," said Shawn. "Mom made me wear them to a football game last year for marching band. They were really heavy, with D batteries in them, but my feet never got cold."

Shawn hurried and got ready. He had all kinds of layers on and he had packets that were hand warmers in his pockets, if his hands got too cold.

"Pray for me," said Shawn, as he walked out to the garage. Jenna put on all of the winter clothing again and went with him. They stood there a long time, trying to figure it all out. Shawn took the end of the rope and wound it two times around a metal support for the garage door opener and knotted it. Then he picked up the rope and put it next to Jenna.

"As I move, slowly give me rope," instructed Shawn. "If I reach the end of the rope, pull it really hard, leaving it attached to the pole. I guess you will know I found the bus if I stop pulling the rope."

"What will you do if you reach the bus," asked Jenna.

"I'll try to tie the rope onto the bus somehow, maybe onto a mirror or something," said Shawn.

"OK, I'll hold the rope and feed it to you very slowly," said Jenna.

"We will figure it out," said Shawn.

Jenna was bundled up like Shawn and she had a scarf around her neck and face, with just a slit to peek out. She was amazed at how dark it was outside, considering it was only 1:00 pm. The wind made a howling noise that never stopped and the snow was never ending. She estimated the snow to be more than two feet deep and she wondered how Shawn would be able to walk through it. Snow was really blowing into the garage. Troubling thoughts went through her mind as she slowly released rope. *What if Shawn gets stuck in the snow? What if he doesn't come back? What if the kids wreck the house or get hurt? How did I get in such a mess? But this is so much better than sitting at home all alone, waiting for my parents to get home. Now that was a hopeless life.*

Shawn regretted coming out the minute he left. He was exhausted by the time he got past his grandparents' house, but he kept going. Shawn thought he could see a slight dip in the snow where he had walked home, and he followed that. After a while, Shawn checked his watch and he had been walking fifty-five minutes. He knew that he should be getting close to the school bus, but he could only see about six feet ahead of himself.

Shawn took a huge step, and his boot came off. He found himself stepping down through the snow with his stocking foot. He twisted his body around to find his boot and lost his balance. He fell hard onto the snow. It was no small matter getting the boot back on and standing up. The entire foot episode cost him another fifteen minutes, and now his boot was crammed with snow.

Shawn was so uncomfortable and discouraged that he considered turning around and going back home. He was also feeling weak and hungry. *Why didn't I eat something when we were feeding those little kids?* Shawn thought. *I will stick with this another five or ten minutes and if I don't find a bus, I'm turning around.* But then he thought he could see something big ahead of him. It didn't look yellow, like a school bus, but it was big. The blowing snow made it so difficult to see anything, but finally he reached the big structure and it was the school bus. Shawn took the rope and tied it onto the rear-view mirror. It took him a minute to pry the door open, but when he did, he couldn't believe his eyes. The driver appeared to be unconscious, with her head tipped back and her mouth open. The children were huddled together in little groups to keep warm.

"What happened to your bus driver?" Shawn asked.

"We think she died," said a tiny little girl.

Shawn leaned down close to the driver, and she was breathing very rapidly. "No, she's alive," said Shawn. "It's just too noisy to hear her breathing." The roar of the storm was deafening.

"I shut off the engine," said a boy. "I was afraid the snow was above the exhaust pipe."

"Well that was really smart of you," said Shawn. "What is your name?"

"Zach," said the boy.

"Did any of you try to use the radio?" asked Shawn.

"We couldn't get it to work," said Zach.

Shawn walked through the bus. Several of the children were asleep and he hoped they weren't suffering from hypothermia. He thought he should try to get through to the bus garage. After messing with the phone for a while, he finally got through.

Shawn said, "Hello, this is Shawn Workman. I was with Angie when you told her about the missing bus. Well, I managed to get here, and I'm sorry to tell you that the bus driver is in a bad way."

"What do you mean?" asked Ray.

"She can't talk and she is barely conscious," answered Shawn.

"What about the children?" Ray asked.

Shawn said, "Some of them seem fine, but others are asleep. I'm a little concerned about them. It's pretty cold in here."

"Wake them up Shawn. Get them moving and help them warm up," said Ray.

"I'll do that Ray. And maybe you can think of a way to get some help here," Shawn said.

Shawn walked through the bus and said, "My name is Shawn. Your bus driver is very sick and we want to get help for her. But first we need to see how you guys are doing. I want you all to stand up and let me look at you."

The little boys and girls woke up, and stood up for Shawn. The little ones started crying and asking for their mommies, and they complained about being cold. Shawn had them sit close together in the middle of the bus, with the older ones putting their arm around the little ones, for comfort as well as warmth. Shawn looked out the windows, but he couldn't see anything but snow.

"Do any of you know where we are? Do you remember dropping off any kids before your bus driver got sick?" asked Shawn.

A little girl said, "My friend Olivia went to get off the bus and her daddy came up to the bus and got her. Then Phyllis closed the door and started acting funny, and put her head back like that."

The bus phone rang and Shawn answered it. Ray said, "We don't know how to help you Shawn. We are trying to get the fire department to help, but we don't know where you are."

"One of the children said that they dropped off a little girl named Olivia, and that her father came up to the bus to get her, and then the bus driver closed the door and then had her problem," said Shawn.

"Now that could be very helpful," said Ray. "I'll call you right back."

Shawn reminded the bigger children to take care of the little ones. He had to yell because the winds were so loud. Then he turned to the bus driver. He pulled off her glove and took hold of her right hand. "One of the children called you Phyllis. Is that your name?" The bus driver did not seem to respond, but she was looking right at Shawn and breathing rapidly. He put her glove back on her hand and tried her left hand. He repeated, "Is your name Phyllis?" This time she squeezed Shawn's hand.

Suddenly Shawn was startled when someone knocked on the bus door. He opened the door and a man and two teenage boys came in, covered with snow.

The man said, "Hi. I just got a call from the bus garage, telling me that your bus might still be at our driveway. I couldn't believe it. That was like two hours ago that Olivia got dropped off. We are going to get you all into the house."

"OK boys and girls. We are getting help from Olivia's family," said Shawn.

The man, who said his name was Brad Snow, and his two sons each took one child and carried them out the bus door. For what seemed like hours, they moved the children into the house. Finally Mr. Snow and one of his sons carried the bus driver into the house. The family invited Shawn to stay with them instead of going home. It was dark and cool inside because the power was out, so Shawn decided to warm up a little and then go home.

Once inside the Snow's house, Shawn called the bus garage and told Ray that all the children and the bus driver were now inside Olivia's house.

"Thank you Shawn. All of the children in the district are safe now, so we can all finally relax. You are hero Shawn. Good job!"

Shawn mumbled, "Well thank you sir."

Then Ray said, "Oh, and expect that phone to start ringing. Those parents are going to need to talk to their kids."

The adults in the house insisted that Shawn spend the night with them, but Shawn told them that he needed to get home. He called his house and told Angie that he found the other bus, and asked her to have Jenna come in and talk to him. It took her a few minutes, and he worried about her as he waited.

"Hello, Shawn?" asked Jenna.

"Yes, it's me," Shawn answered. "Are you OK? Were you out in the garage all this time? Are you freezing?"

"I'm OK. What happened?" Jenna asked.

"I'll tell you all about it when I get home, but so you know, everything is good. If the rope is still tied onto the garage, I'm coming home," said Shawn.

"The rope is just like you left it," said Jenna. "But I'll go back out and secure the extra rope, so it's tight. Oh Shawn, are you sure you should go back out there?"

"I'm sure," said Shawn. "I want to get home, and go to Grandma and Grandpa's warm house, curl up in bed, and sleep until the snow melts." They hung up because both phones had calls coming in.

When Jenna was off the phone, she went out and secured the extra length of rope that Shawn had not needed. When she came back inside, Angie expressed some concerns. They were out of milk and hot chocolate powder and popcorn and hot dogs. What were they going to feed all of these children? And these children were getting very cold and cranky.

Then Angie noticed something. "Hey," she said. "Why are the lights on next door and not here?"

Jenna told Angie what Shawn had just said about going next door to their grandparent's warm house. The power had been out for an hour and the temperature inside was dropping fast.

"My grandparents' phone number must be here someplace," Jenna said.

"Why don't you ask one of the twins?" suggested Angie. "Where are the twins? I haven't seen them since I walked them into the house hours ago."

"I'll go find them," said Jenna. Upstairs, she found the boys in their room. It was pretty dark in there, but Jenna could see them curled up on one of their beds, sound asleep, with a heavy comforter over them. Next to them was a pile of wrappers by a plastic pumpkin. She had to laugh. No wonder they weren't hungry. They must have finished off all of their Halloween candy.

"Drew. Will. Wake up. We need to call Grandma and Grandpa next door. Do you know their number?" Jenna asked.

"It's on the refrigerator with all of the important numbers," said Will.

"You guys need to wake up now or you'll be awake all night," said Jenna. "Come downstairs, and dress warmly, because the power is off and it's getting cold inside."

Jenna ran downstairs and called her grandparents next door. She explained all about the children they were watching.

"You need to bring the children here," said Grandpa. "We have a wonderful fireplace and a generator that can keep us going for days. We are always prepared for emergencies. And we have lots of food."

The children were not happy about putting on their winter clothes and going back outside, but Angie told them it will be much better next door. Jenna took them in groups as they found their coats and bundled up. Finally Angie brought in the last little ones. They had all of the children sit down in the family room, which had the fireplace. They fed the children and dug out many blankets and quilts and bedspreads to make beds for all the children. Angie remembered to call Ray and give him the new number where the children can be reached.

Lesley ran into Cheryl's room and shouted, "My kids are safe and your son Shawn is the one who rescued them!"

"What?" asked Cheryl.

"Marilyn just called me," said Lesley. "She said that Ray called from the bus garage to tell me that Zach and Zoe are safe. And then she told me that your son Shawn went out in the snow and found the missing bus. Their bus driver had a stroke, so Shawn, with the help of a little girl on the bus, figured out that they were right outside a kid's house. Here is the number where I can reach them and talk to them."

"I can't believe he would go back out in the storm," said Cheryl.

"Well, I'm so glad he did. He's a hero. I want to call the kids now," said Lesley. They ran to the phone and called.

"Hello, this is the Snow residence. Did you want to talk to one of the children?" asked Mr. Snow.

Lesley talked to Zach and Zoe, and was very relieved to hear their voices. Then Cheryl asked if she could talk to Shawn. Lesley told Mr. Snow that Shawn's mother would like to talk to him.

"I'm sorry," Mr. Snow answered. "Shawn insisted that he needed to get home and that the trip back would be fine. He's been gone for about 15 minutes."

Lesley could tell that Cheryl heard what he said, because she sat down and put her head down. She got off the phone and sat down with Cheryl.

"I wonder if Jenna went out in the storm too," said Cheryl. "This day will never end." Lesley knew they needed to get back with their classes, but she put her arm around Cheryl.

"Let's go back to class and get the kids settled," said Lesley. "Give Shawn time to get home."

Chapter 7

Cheryl went back to her room, just as her class was returning to her room, probably to spend the next ten hours or more.

"You aren't going to make us work, are you, Mrs. Workman?" asked Michael.

Cheryl laughed and said, "Are you kidding? Then I would have more papers to grade. No, we are starting our snow party in ten minutes. Now you guys go to the restroom, and call your parents if you like, and then we will begin our first game."

"What game?" asked Eddie.

"We're starting off with Phase Ten," said Cheryl. "Trust me, you'll love it!"

Mrs. Johnson, Eddie's mom came in. "Well, I would rather go home, but since I can't, I'm thankful to be in your cozy little room, Mrs. Workman," she said.

"Please call me Cheryl. I'm thankful that I have this class for the night. Just between you and me, it's my favorite. And I'm thankful you'll be with us. We can make it fun."

Cheryl and Eddie's mom pushed the desks together, making a table of sorts in the middle of the room.

Suddenly Eddie rushed into the room. "Mom, I just got a text from Carter," he said. "It's not good."

"What wrong?" asked his mom.

"Well look at it for yourself," said Eddie, as he put his phone up for his mom to read.

The message read: "Stupid me went to mailbox im lost help." Eddie's mom looked up at everyone, obviously in shock.

"Maybe he's kidding," suggested Cheryl.

Eddie's mom grabbed her phone out of her purse and called her neighbor. "Jayne, isn't Carter there in the house with you and Jerod?"

"Last time I looked, they were playing video games," said Jayne.

"Would you just look in on them?" asked Eddie's mom.

Seconds later, Jayne came back on the phone. "Jerod is still playing games, but he thought Carter just went to the bathroom. He's doesn't seem to be around."

Cheryl thought the distraught mom was going to pass out. "Are you alright?" she asked.

Eddie's mom, still on the phone, got herself together and explained to her neighbor that Carter might have gone out to their mailbox and that he could be lost out there.

"OK," said Jayne. "I'm just going to see if there are still tracks in the snow. I'll call you back."

"Jayne, don't......." said Eddie's mom, but her neighbor had already hung up.

"Why would your boy go out to the mailbox?" asked Cheryl.

"Carter is expecting a new video game to arrive," she answered. "Since we live next door, he probably thought he could get there and back quickly. I'm sure the mail truck didn't even go out today, but he wouldn't think of that."

"Mom, I'm going to text Carter, and tell him to follow his tracks back to the house," said Eddie.

"No," said his mom. "Let me call him." She took her phone and called Carter. It rang and rang and he didn't answer.

"You know how loud the storm is in this heavy building," said Cheryl. "I'm sure he just can't hear his phone."

Tears ran down the mother's face. Eddie walked away from her and grabbed Michael just as he was coming into the room and pulled him back out into the hallway.

"Oh dear," said Eddie's mom. "People can freeze to death out in the storm."

Most of the students had returned to Cheryl's classroom. Cheryl moved the desks apart and turned them to face the front of the room.

"What are you doing," asked Mark. "I thought we were going to play games."

"Change of plans," said Cheryl. "I'm putting a movie in for now. I can't concentrate on games when there is so much going on."

Cheryl put in a movie and turned down the lights. The kids plopped into their seats and were instantly tuned in to the movie. Cheryl went over to where Eddie's mom was standing, staring at her phone.

"I wonder why Eddie and Michael aren't here by now," said Cheryl. "They are usually all about games."

Just then Eddie's mom's phone rang. "It's Carter," she shouted. "Hello, Carter?"

"Mom, I'm OK," said Carter.

"Oh, thank you God. Thank you," said his mom.

"Mom, Jerod's mom did something really smart," said Carter. "You know Jerod's dad is a volunteer fireman. Well, she opened the garage door and turned on the flashers and the siren, and I saw them and heard them, and walked that way. It took me a long time, but I made it."

"Please, thank her for me Son, and whatever you do, don't go outside again until I come and get you myself," said his mom.

"I promise Mom," said Carter. "And tell Eddie that I'm alright. I tried to call him first, but he didn't answer his phone."

Once Eddie's mom hung up, Cheryl asked, "I wonder where Eddie and Michael are? I told everyone to be back in ten minutes. Would you call Eddie?"

Eddie's mom tried to call him, but he didn't answer. She walked over to her purse to put her phone away and discovered that her keys were missing. "Oh no," she said. "I have a very bad feeling. My keys are missing. I hope Eddie didn't go out alone to find Carter. He's very protective of his little brother."

"He's probably not alone," said Cheryl. "Michael is missing too. But how would they even find the car in this mess? All the cars look alike by now, and they are buried in snow. And I'm sure they aren't plowing out the parking lot."

"I always park in the same place and Eddie knows that," said Eddie's mom. "I'm just going to run around to that exit. I parked right next to the door."

"Don't let the door close behind you, Mrs. Johnson," shouted Cheryl. "All the exits are locked."

Cheryl was still worried about Shawn. With the kids watching the movie, and Mrs. Johnson gone to look for Eddie and Michael, she ran to the back of the room and called home. No one answered. That was strange, considering they had a houseful of people, although they were mostly kids. She decided to call next door to see if her parents knew anything.

Jenna was the one who answered the phone.

"Jenna," said Cheryl. "Have you heard from Shawn? They told me he went back out in the storm."

"He just got here Aunt Cheryl," said Jenna. "He's fine."

"Let me talk to him," said Cheryl.

"Hi Mom," said Shawn. "I know what you're going to say."

"First of all," said Cheryl. "I'm very proud of you. I understand that you saved a lot of lives today. But why didn't you stay put at the house with those people who asked you to stay? Why would you go out again? I've been really worried."

"I'm sorry Mom," said Shawn. "I was just so hungry and wet and cold, and all I could think about was going home, changing clothes, and then going to Grandma's for some good food and their warm house. They didn't have any power at that house."

"Well, are you OK now?" asked Cheryl. "I guess our house has no power either."

"Yes, Jenna and Angie got all the kids to Grandma and Grandpa's. I changed clothes and locked up the house, but I'm starving," said Shawn. "So can I go now and eat something?"

"Yes, but I mean it, Shawn," said Cheryl. "From now on, leave the rescuing to others."

"I never want to go out in the cold again," said Shawn.

"OK," said Cheryl. "Get some food and then get some rest."

Eddie's mom looked out the exit door that was closest to her car, and the snow was blowing so furiously that she couldn't see her car. She had no choice, but to go out and look closer, so she asked a student to wait at the door for her. But when she pushed on the door, it didn't move. The snow was piled high against the door. *Well the boys didn't go out this door*, she thought. She hurried toward the front doors and there were both boys, arguing with the custodian, who wouldn't let them out the door.

"Boys," shouted Eddie's mom. "Carter is safe and back in the house. Now get back to your room and I'll tell you all about it when I get there."

Once the boys were out of sight, she talked to Ralph, the custodian. He said the boys were determined to charge out of the building and look for a car. "I told them that once they got away from the covered area, the snow was over three feet deep. They said they didn't care and they would get through."

"Well I can't thank you enough for keeping them in the building. Eddie was worried about his little brother, and his buddy Michael would do anything for him, so I can only imagine how they tried to get past you," said Mrs. Johnson.

"You're right about that, but even though they were frustrated, the boys were respectful, and didn't disobey me," said Ralph.

"I'm thankful for that," said Eddie's mom, and she gave him a quick hug and went back to the classroom.

Chapter 8

Back at the grandparents' house, Jenna and Shawn were exhausted from the rescue mission and ordered by Grandma to retreat to the den to warm up and rest. But first she gave them some leftover pizza that she had warmed up and kept hidden from all of the children.

"I'm really happy to be here, with my family, and to have something worthwhile to do," said Jenna. "But what a long, cold, exhausting day!"

"Actually, I'm a little concerned about my fingers," said Shawn. "I had those pocket warmers, but I never got a chance to put my hands in my pockets. I hope I don't have frost bite. They really hurt."

"I put the rope under my arm to keep it tight," said Jenna, "so I kept my hands in my pockets, inside a pair of warm gloves. Let me see your hands." She took hold of his hands and they were very cold. Very gently, she massaged his hands and fingers.

"Do you know what?" said Shawn. "My hands actually feel a little better now." They ate the pizza and drank some hot chocolate that Grandpa had delivered to the room.

"Do you think we could watch the TV," asked Jenna. "The little kids can't hear it in here and I would like to know what's going on outside."

Shawn found a local station, and the news was on. The newscasters were explaining that they had been on job since they arrived at the station at 5:00 am for the morning show.

"Look at those three news people," said Shawn. "They look terrible."

"Well, it sounds like their day has been as rough as our day," said Jenna. "You and I have looked better."

Shawn heard something on the TV that caught his interest and he motioned to Jenna to watch. The newscasters were sharing a local story about the storm.

"And now after all that bad news about widespread power outages, transportation at a complete standstill, and many deaths in our city alone, we have one heart-warming story about two cousins responsible for saving the lives of 46 elementary school children stranded on two school busses," shared the lady newscaster.

The male newscaster continued as two snapshots appeared on the TV. "Jenna Ashcraft and Shawn Workman, two eighteen- year- old first cousins, used their brains and their brawn to rescue 46 little school children who were sure to freeze to death. First Jenna suggested and invited 24 children from a school bus into their house, and helped the bus driver, Angie Knight, lead and carry the precious little ones inside."

"And then, when the cousins were informed that there was another stranded school bus nearby, they rigged up a rope, and Shawn went and found the bus. He saved the lives of another 22 children," relayed the lady newscaster. "The parents of these 46 children can sleep peacefully tonight," said the newscaster, "knowing their children are being fed and nurtured in two homes."

Philip Johnson, superintendent of Longfellow Local Schools, commented that the school system is thankful for the ingenuity of these two brave individuals, and for their grandparents, Fred and Evelyn Jones, and for Brad and Jessica Snow, who are caring for all of those children tonight."

Shawn turned the sound down when he saw the shock on Jenna's face. "What's wrong?"

"I had no idea," said Jenna. "I just thought Angie took my picture because she wanted to remember me. What if my parents somehow see that?"

"That's unlikely," said Shawn, "since they are in Rome."

"I can't believe I did something to make the news," said Jenna. "I just need a few more days of peace and quiet before they find out where I am. Is that too much to ask?"

"You consider today a day of peace and quiet?" asked Shawn.

"Yes," said Jenna. "Being here with my family, that I didn't even know existed, doing something worthwhile, and working on it with others, was unbelievably satisfying. I haven't had this much freedom my whole life. They always told me where I could go and what I could do, and it wasn't very much. I have always been made to feel like a failure and a reject. I felt like a little mouse. Today, I feel capable. And I don't want those two, poor excuses for parents, to take this away from me."

Jenna and Shawn slept for a couple hours in the den and woke up wondering how it was going in the family room with all of those children.

In the cozy family room of Fred and Evelyn Jones, all of the children were sound asleep except a sweet little red-headed girl. Evelyn finally invited the little girl to climb up on her lap and go to sleep. Drew and Will had their own bedroom upstairs, so they were enjoying a private night's sleep. Shawn and Jenna were happy to see all of the sleeping children. They sat down to have a quiet visit with their grandparents and Angie, the bus driver.

"I just peeked out the window," said Shawn. "I thought it would have quit snowing by now, but it's still coming down. Jenna, we should have listened to the weather forecast."

"They don't know what this storm is going to do," said Fred. "Only God knows that!"

"I just wish we were all here together," said Shawn. "Poor mom is at the school with all those kids. And Josh and Susan are at the high school. That can't be comfortable, sleeping on a classroom floor with a bunch of rowdy high school kids. And Dad is sleeping at his hardware store."

"I know," said Evelyn. "I don't think the schools have generators. They are probably very cold by now."

"Dad doesn't have a generator," said Shawn. "And where is he going to sleep?"

"Your dad probably sells generators at his store," said Fred. "So don't worry about him. We have so much to be thankful for. We are all inside and we are all safe. Some people aren't so fortunate."

Shawn and Jenna told their grandparents about the news report that they were featured in. Shawn shared, "Jenna is very upset that her picture is out there, and that her parents might see it and know that she is up here with all of us.

"Don't worry about it Sweetie," said Grandpa. "You are eighteen and they can't do a thing. You are here with us, forever."

Angie changed the subject and spoke up. "Ray at our bus garage, said that we didn't lose any lives in our school district, except for Phyllis. And she might have died even without the storm. He said that after we got the kids safely inside, he thought it was such a good idea that he had the others do the same."

"Other schools weren't so lucky," said Shawn. "We were just listening to the news. There were thousands of deaths in the Northeast today, and among them were school children on stranded busses."

"Oh Dear Lord," said Evelyn, as she looked down at the precious little girl in her arms. "Lord, please comfort all of those people who have lost loved ones. And if there are any people out there in danger, please keep them safe."

Fred picked up the prayer where Evelyn left off. "And Father, if it's in your will, please move this storm out to sea, and melt all of this snow. In Jesus' name, Amen."

"Amen," said Shawn.

Jenna didn't know what to think. Finally she asked, "So you all believe there's a god someplace, and he hears you talking right here in the living room?"

"Didn't your mom ever pray?" asked Evelyn. "We raised her better than that."

"No," said Fred. "She never accepted Jesus as her savior. She got involved with those uppity kids and quit going to church. It didn't make sense to force her. Remember. We tried to get her to go to events at church, thinking it would get her going to worship services. Nothing worked."

"I know," said Evelyn. "I always thought she would go back when she had a child."

"They never took me to church," said Jenna. "Last Sunday was the first time I ever went to a church."

Fred jumped up and went to a bookshelf. "Here you go Jenna. I barely used this Bible. I needed large print as soon as I bought it. Start reading it. Start in the beginning and then tell me what you think every now and then. I'll tell you when to switch to the New Testament."

"The New Testament? Is that another Bible?" asked Jenna. She saw Shawn laugh.

"No Jenna," said Evelyn. "The Bible is divided into the Old and New Testament. You'll figure it out very quickly."

Jenna looked at her new red Bible and said, "Well, I'll try to find time to read it."

Chapter 9

Harold and Cynthia Ashcraft had finished five days of their Rome vacation, having the time of their life. Now they were headed south to the city of Naples on a tour bus. Cynthia and her new friend Stephany were sharing a bottle of wine, and everything they talked about was incredibly funny. They were getting a little out of control, but the husbands had already passed out.

"You are lucky not to have any kids," said Stephany. "I'm paying a fortune to the babysitter."

"Oh we have a daughter," said Cynthia. "She's just old enough to leave at home. She's of age; she just doesn't know it." She started giggling again.

"I don't get it," said Stephany. "She doesn't know her own age?"

"Well, when she was little, we kind of forgot her age and told her she was four, when she was already five," said Cynthia. "I guess we were a little drunk. And then, we didn't want to bother with the kindergarten routine, so we just left her in day care another year."

"So you lied to her all these years?" asked Stephany.

"Yes. Right now, she's probably sitting on the floor in her bedroom, feeling sorry for herself," said Cynthia laughing.

"Well, you aren't going to get the mother-of-the-year award," said Stephany. "But you are a lot of fun to hang out with."

Something Stephany said made Cynthia angry, although she couldn't remember what it was. She drank another glass of wine and turned her back on her companion. Suddenly the bus began to shake

52

and swerve. The bus driver was shouting something about the road moving. He put his foot on the brake and tried to pull to the curb. A tree fell right in front of the bus, and they crashed into it, sending the passengers onto the floor and into the aisles. People were screaming and crying, and the bus was still shaking very powerfully. Someone shouted that it was an earthquake.

Harold woke up on the floor on top of Jeffrey, Stephany's husband. Harold's head was banging into the back of a seat like a wood pecker, and he couldn't stop it. Cynthia probably had a broken arm from the impact, and her face was badly bruised. She saw Harold on the floor and wanted to help him, but the shaking continued. Up and down, back and forth, it went on and on. Finally the shaking stopped, and the people on the bus were screaming and crying.

"Harold, get up and get me off this bus!" shouted Cynthia. Harold just put his hands on his head and moaned.

"Get up Harold," shouted Cynthia again. Cynthia noticed Stephany on the floor, unconscious and bleeding, so she slid down the seat to avoid stepping on her. She grabbed Harold's hand with her good arm, and tried to get his attention. People were still screaming and wailing. Harold looked up at Cynthia, barely able to focus. And she said, "Harold, we need to get off this bus!"

Cynthia knew enough about earthquakes to know that she did not want to be slammed around on that bus any more when the aftershocks come. She pulled Harold's arm and this time he seemed to wake up.

"Let go of me a minute so I can get myself up," said Harold. Finally he was able to move off of Jeffrey enough to put his hands on the floor of the bus, and finally wiggle out onto the floor and pull himself up. He put his arm around Cynthia, and together they went down the aisle of the bus, stepping on and around people, who were reaching out to them and begging for help. Finally they reached the door of the bus.

"Where are you two going?" asked the tour guide. His forehead was bleeding profusely. "We all need to stay together."

"We are getting off this bus," said Harold.

"That's not a good idea!" said the tour guide. "We are waiting for an ambulance."

"We will feel safer outside the bus," said Cynthia. Just as they stepped down on the road, the earth began to shake again. Harold and Cynthia sat right down on the side of the road, and were shaken back and forth and bounced up and down, until they were very dizzy and disoriented.

Cynthia began throwing up. Tears ran down her cheeks and she began shaking.

"Harold, my arm hurts," said Cynthia. "I think we'd better get to a hospital."

"Oh I don't know Dearest," said Harold. "The roads are really clogged both ways. Look at the road on the other side of that tree. We aren't going anywhere and no one is getting to us for a while."

"I'm being punished for being a lousy mom, Harold," said Cynthia.

"But you don't believe in God, Dear," said Harold. "So who could be punishing you?"

"Oh Harold. I do believe in God," said Cynthia. "I've just been ignoring him for a long time. Now he's punishing me."

"Don't be ridiculous. God didn't cause this earthquake to punish you," said Harold. "We will get you to a hospital eventually. Do you have any pain killers with you?"

"No I don't have anything. Harold I feel terrible," said Cynthia. She threw up again and her broken arm fell limply at her side, causing her to scream.

"You know something Cynthia?" asked Harold. "I don't feel very well either. My head feels like it's been in a boxing match. Let's stay right here and wait for some help."

Then the earth began to shake again, and Harold and Cynthia passed out.

At the middle school, Cheryl's class decided to just talk for a while after dinner. The classroom was dimly lit, since the main power was off in the building and the emergency lights weren't very bright. The temperature inside the building was dropping, so they all had their coats, hats, and gloves on, but that didn't bother them. They were having fun just hanging out together.

"School will be cancelled tomorrow, don't you think?" asked Eddie.

"It's so bad out there," said Eddie's mom, "that we probably won't have school until after Thanksgiving."

Cheryl said, "I just hope we don't have to stay here that whole time!"

"As long as we don't have to do work, I wouldn't mind," said Michael.

"Well I would mind," said Cheryl. "Thanksgiving is always special to me, but this year it is extra special. Our family has something amazing to be thankful for."

"What is it?" asked Eddie's mom.

"I have a sister named Cynthia who hasn't spoken to my mom, dad, me, or any of the family for around twenty years," said Cheryl.

Melissa, family friend of Eddie and his mom, said, "So she finally called and she's coming for Thanksgiving."

"No, that's not going to happen," said Cheryl. "But it turns out that Cynthia and her husband are terrible parents. Their daughter, Jenna, discovered that she had grandparents and traveled across the country by bus to find them. She didn't even know that she had aunts and uncles and cousins. We love her, and she loves us, and she's never going back. We are so very thankful to God for bringing us together."

"I'm surprised her parents let her come," said Eddie's mom.

"Well that's an interesting story," said Cheryl. She shared with them about Jenna's parents' trip to Rome, and they were all pretty sympathetic.

"My birth parents were like that, always putting their own pleasure ahead of Carter and me," said Eddie. "The luckiest day of our lives was when we were removed from them and placed with my forever mom and dad." He jumped up and gave his mom a long hug. Even in the dimly lit room, everyone knew his mom was crying.

That night the students stayed in a dark, cool middle school. Cheryl kept her door locked and she covered the tiny window in the door. They ignored banging on the door a few times. Cheryl, Eddie's mother, and the small group of nine students talked until midnight, and agreed that they would sleep until at least 8 am the next morning. When necessary, they went in groups to the restroom. The only contact they were to make was with their parents on their cell phones.

At 8:30 in the morning, Cheryl's cell phone vibrated. She looked at it and a call was coming from her friend Kinsey. She certainly couldn't ignore her call.

"Hi Kinsey," said Cheryl. "Did you have a good night?"

"No, I did not," said Kinsey. "Since I don't have a first period class, they had me spend the night helping Geoffrey in his classroom of 32 wild and disrespectful students. I just escaped for a while to my own room. I locked the door and I'm checking my wounds."

"You're injured?" asked Cheryl.

"Yes," said Kinsey. "I got elbowed in the face early in the night, and have a black eye. They were just being wild at that point, although I never got an apology."

"You said wounds?" asked Cheryl.

"Oh yeah, there are more," said Kinsey. "I was trying to break up a fight between two girls. I'm sure you've heard of Rachel and Lauren. Lauren had Rachel on the floor and was punching her face, and I tried to grab her arm. She didn't even look at me. She grabbed my arm and pulled me hard. I landed on the floor, after bouncing off a desk. I'm bruised and sore on the whole right side of my body. And I hurt my bad knee, so I'm limping too."

"What did they do to them?" asked Cheryl.

"Both girls spent the night in the principal's office," said Kinsey. "They weren't allowed to talk at all."

"Didn't that settle things down for the rest of the night?" asked Cheryl.

"Not really," said Kinsey. "I think they were just so scared about the snow and the cold weather. Acting out is how they are dealing with it. I can seriously say that was the worst night of my life."

"Have you heard anything about the weather?" asked Cheryl.

"Well, the sun is out and it's not snowing," said Kinsey. "I want to go home so badly, and soak my poor, miserable body in a tub of hot water."

"What if we have to spend another night here?" asked Cheryl.

"I'll kill myself," said Kinsey. "I do have some good news. Remember how I was so worried about my mom and dad? Well, they didn't go out at all, because they heard the weather forecast. They were having a wonderful time watching an I Love Lucy Marathon on TV, and they weren't even watching it snow. They checked their phones and saw all of the messages and called me. Even without that stress, I can't take another night in that classroom."

"If we have to spend another night here, you can lock yourself in the room with my class," said Cheryl. "We actually had a good time last night, and then we had a good night's sleep."

"Oh thank you Cheryl," said Kinsey. "Of course I'll have to convince our principal not to make me go in that room again."

"If I were you," said Cheryl, "I wouldn't mention it to him. Just hide in here, and let yourself heal."

Tuesday morning the children woke up in the home of Fred and Evelyn Jones, and the little ones began crying for their mommies.

"Oh no Fred," said Evelyn. "I'm afraid the children aren't going to be entertained so easily today. We need some new ideas."

"Well breakfast will help," said Fred. "Let's get these kids some Lucky Charms."

"Jenna, go get Angie up," said Evelyn. "She's upstairs in the bedroom to the left. These kids need to talk to their parents."

Angie came in looking like she didn't sleep all night. "Jenna said I need to start calling parents. I don't have their numbers."

"Didn't you keep records?" asked Evelyn.

"Ray at the bus garage gave the parents your number, so the parents called us," said Angie.

"Children have to know their phone number and address in kindergarten, don't they?" asked Jenna. "They can probably all call their mom."

"I hope you're right," said Angie. "Direct me to your phone, and send me the crying kids."

Fred set a bunch of kids down at the table and gave them a bowl of cereal and milk. Then he turned on the TV in the kitchen. The weather man was actually smiling and pointing to a map with a radar display.

"There is finally some good news in the weather department," said the weather man. "The storm has moved away and the sun is out. The temperatures are still around 8 degrees, but they should begin rising soon. Hopefully the snow layers will soon start shrinking." He continued discussing the forecast and the temperatures in the cities across the north.

Jenna came in with another group of children that she thought were ready for breakfast and Fred put them in the dining room. He put bowls in front of them and began feeding them. As he did, he assured the children that they will see their parents soon, since the snow was melting.

Then an interesting story came on the news. The newscaster began talking as a video appeared on the screen. "A severe earthquake shook Italy today in the area between Rome and Naples. The quake registered 8.0 on the Richter scale, leveling high rises in the cities, knocking down bridges and toppling trees on highways, destroying property. Hundreds of people have died of their injuries. Hospitals are full, with thousands waiting in parking lots to get admitted. People in remote areas have little hope of being rescued due to the condition of the roads. Christian organizations around the country are planning mission trips to aid the people of Italy. Donations can be made by calling the number on the screen.

"Are you thinking what I'm thinking?" asked Fred.

"That my parents might be somewhere in that mess," said Jenna.

"Exactly," said Fred. "But it sounds like the quake didn't hit Rome. Why would they leave the city? They are probably fine."

"If there is action someplace, Mother and Father are sure to be there," said Jenna. "They thrive on drama."

"You don't seem very worried about them," said Fred.

"When I was little, I worried a lot, that they wouldn't come home, and I would be left alone," said Jenna. "As I got older, I hoped they wouldn't come home. Do you think I'm a terrible person?"

"No Sweetie. I don't blame you. Say, did you get a chance yet to read any of your new Bible," asked Fred.

"No," said Jenna. "I was just so exhausted last night."

Just then there was a loud knocking on the door. "Who could that be?" asked Fred. He went to the front door and there stood a young couple, four feet up on the snow pile. He helped them get in the door. They took off their snow shoes and stepped into the room.

"I'm Rodney Matthews and this is my wife April. We came to see our children and take them home as soon as we can."

"Mommy," shouted a little girl with messy, brown pigtails, who came charging into the room and jumped into her mom's arms.

"Oh I missed you so much last night," said April Matthews.

"I missed you too Mommy, but I didn't cry," said the little girl. "Ethan didn't cry either."

"And where is Ethan?" asked Rodney Matthews.

"He's in there Daddy," said Sophia, pointing to the living room. They went in the living room and Ethan was sitting on the floor with a large group of children, watching an Alvin and the Chipmunks movie. Rodney called to his son.

"Oh Hi Dad. Hi Mom. What's new?" said Ethan. Then he looked back at the movie.

The Matthews couple started laughing. "We were picturing the kids crying and scared," said Rodney. "Instead we find them having a slumber party and watching cartoons."

"Do we have to go home now?" asked Sophia. "I'm in the next group to have breakfast."

"No Honey," said April. "We don't have four sets of snow shoes, so we'll be here for a while. Can we help you folks?"

"Oh, and can we chip in to pay for all this food you're providing?" asked Rodney Matthews.

"Yes, to the help," said Fred. "We're a little outnumbered. But we don't need any money. We keep extra food in the house for just a time as this. We like to be prepared for anything."

So Rodney and April Matthews stayed and helped feed and entertain the children at the Jones's home.

Cynthia woke up, and it was light outside. She was on the floor of the bus, next to a sleeping Harold, and they were moving. She looked around and noticed the tour guide looking at her and smiling.

"How did we get back on the bus?" Cynthia asked the tour guide.

"Bob here, our driver, decided to try starting the bus, and to his surprise, it started right up," said Skip the tour guide. "The only thing keeping us from backing up and turning around, were your two bodies. So we managed to get you both up and back on the bus. We are on our way back to Rome. We haven't felt any aftershocks since we left the area."

"We need medical treatment," said Cynthia.

"Who doesn't," said Skip. "I'm not even sure everyone on this bus is still alive. We are going straight to the emergency room."

Once they were in the ER, Harold and Cynthia were put on a waiting list, and warned that it could be hours before they get checked out by a doctor. They decided to curl up together, making sure to prop up their injured limbs and cradle their heads. Just as they were about to drop back to sleep, they heard something interesting on the television.

The reporter was describing The Great American Blizzard, the snow storms that covered all of the central and northeast states in the US. Harold and Cynthia heard all of that and could care less. But the name Jenna Ashcraft caught their attention. They strained to look at the TV to see the face of a girl who had the same name as their daughter. To their surprise, the girl in the photo looked a lot like their Jenna. How could that be?

"What did they say about first cousins? What state did they say they were in?" asked Cynthia.

"I think they said something about school busses," said Harold. "That girl in the picture must just be a look-alike."

"Oh, you're probably right," said Cynthia. "Even if she somehow managed to get across the country to another state, she wouldn't have anything to do with a school bus. And she's such a mousy girl, she wouldn't be described as some kind of hero."

"Too true, My Sweet," said Harold. "Let's go back to sleep."

"Yes Harold," said Cynthia, as she was falling asleep, "there must be thirty or forty girls named Jenna Ashcraft in our country."

Harold and Cynthia went back to sleep and didn't give the newscast another thought.

Chapter 10

Conditions in the northern part of the country did not improve immediately just because the sun was shining. The temperatures were still hovering around 10 degrees. Cheryl, Lesley, Kinsey, and the other teachers were still stuck at school with the students all day Tuesday and Tuesday night.

The grandparents were still watching many little children at their house, with the help of Jenna and Shawn, Angie the bus driver, and Rodney and April Matthews, who arrived that morning on snow shoes. Monday, the children had been scared and were missing their parents, but Tuesday, they were comfortable at the Jones's home and were getting more difficult to watch. Late in the day, Will and Drew begged Shawn to take them back to their house next door. It was cold and dark there, since the power was still off, but the peace and quiet sounded so good to Shawn, that he agreed to take them.

Finally, at ten o'clock at night, the children were finally all asleep. "Jenna," asked Grandpa, "Did you get an opportunity today to look through your Bible?"

"I did," answered Jenna. "I got away by myself for a couple hours today, while Shawn helped with the kids. I guess the kids really wore him out. But I read the first eleven chapters of Genesis. Do you believe all of that really happened? Were those real people?"

"Oh yes," said Grandpa. "Many of those people are mentioned by Jesus and the disciples in the New Testament."

"And do you believe that we all descended from Adam and Eve?" asked Jenna.

Even though Grandma had little boys curled up on each side of her, she had the Bible on her phone handy. "Listen to this from Acts, chapter 17, starting with verse 24.

'The God who made the world and everything in it is the Lord of heaven and earth and does not live in temples built by human hands. And he is not served by human hands, as if he needed anything. Rather, he himself gives everyone life and breath and everything else. From one man he made all the nations, that they should inhabit the whole earth; and he marked out their appointed times in history and the boundaries of their lands.'"

"So God determined long ago, that I would live in New Jersey in this very year?" asked Jenna.

"Yes," answered Grandma. "But he also knew that you would move to Ohio, and start a brand new life."

"I feel like I still have so much to learn," said Jenna. "But right now I can barely keep my eyes open."

"That's ok Dear," said Grandma. "And tomorrow, hopefully, most of the children will get to go home. The snow plows were able to have some success today on the main roads, so maybe they can get closer to us. I sure hope we can get out and buy a turkey tomorrow, and all the fixings, because the next day is Thanksgiving."

"Would you look at that!" said Grandpa. "There is Shawn in their kitchen and the lights are on. I heard on the radio that the electric company had reached a few neighborhoods."

———

On Wednesday, not only did the sun shine, but the temperatures climbed into the 30's. The snow plows kept making progress, as did the electric company fixing the power. Soon parents were arriving to pick up their children. Around 2:00 in the afternoon, Richie pulled into the driveway, and ran into the grandparent's house with the turkey, potatoes, and all the fixings for Thanksgiving.

"We could have bought all that food, Richie," said Grandpa.

"Well, Cheryl and I were talking this morning, and she wasn't sure how long it would take her to get away from the Middle School or how long until the kids at your house were all picked up. So it seemed best if I go to the store," said Richie. "The grocery store was really busy since people were out of food after being stuck at home so long. They are getting low on supplies, but I managed to get the last two gallons of milk."

"Oh thank you Richie," said Grandma. "We are going to need it tomorrow, if the highways get cleared. And thanks for getting a really big turkey!"

Wednesday evening, Richie, Cheryl, and all their kids, including Jenna, were finally at home together. After dinner, the family gathered in the family room to share their blizzard stories. Drew and Will told some funny stories about playing games with the other kids at Grandma's house. Josh and Susan described their days at the high school as long, cold, dark, and boring. They were given very little freedom, and nothing comfortable to sleep on.

"I had my coat on all the time," said Susan. "And I wore my hat and my hood and my scarf and gloves. I tried sleeping on that cold classroom floor, but the desk was better. I just put my head down on the desk and slept sitting up all night."

"That's what I did too," said Cheryl, "but some of my kids slept on the floor."

Richie did use a generator at his store, and he had grabbed a couple blankets and a pillow on his way out of the house Monday morning, so he was quite comfortable, although very bored, since he had told all his employees not to come in.

Cheryl asked Jenna about her time with her grandparents.

"Grandpa gave me a Bible," said Jenna. "I read the first eleven chapters of Genesis. And that was thanks to Shawn, who watched the kids and let me have a break."

"Jenna," asked Richie. "Do you know anything about Jesus?"

"I know that he is the baby in the manger," said Jenna. "That's about it."

Drew said, "Will and I are only seven, but we know more than that!"

"Did you know that Jesus is God's son and he always has been his son?" asked Will. "He's eternal."

"What?" asked Jenna. "I thought he was born. That's why we celebrate Christmas."

"That's when he came to earth," said Drew. "He lived a perfect life for about thirty-three years. And then he died on the cross for me and everybody else, because we can't be perfect. I mess up all the time, but because of Jesus, I'm forgiven."

"True," said Will. "Drew and I got saved last year. We were baptized!"

"What does that mean?" asked Jenna.

"Wow," said Drew. "You don't know much."

"Boys," said Cheryl. "Jenna never got to go to church her whole life. Her parents never prayed. They never taught her to sing 'Jesus Loves Me' or anything else. She never went to church camp, or Sunday School, or youth group."

"I'm sorry Jenna," said Will. "I didn't know."

"I'm sorry too Jenna," said Drew. "And I'm sorry you never got to go to church."

"Well it's not too late Jenna," said Richie. "You read part of Genesis, so now read something from the New Testament, so you know about the life of Jesus,"

"Well, Christmas is coming Dad," said Josh. "Let's read the first two chapters of Luke together. Then Jenna will know more about Jesus."

"Great idea," said Cheryl. "Everyone go get your pajamas on and brush your teeth. And when we come back, we'll read the Christmas story."

So the family gathered around the table, each with a Bible, and read in Luke about Zechariah and Elizabeth, a very old couple, having a baby who was John the Baptist. Jenna was amazed at the angel visiting Zechariah to tell him about the baby they would have and then an angel came to Mary to tell her that she would have a baby that would be the son of God.

"Jenna, did you notice that Zechariah didn't believe the angel who told him about the baby they would have?" asked Cheryl.

"Well Zechariah paid a big price for his unbelief, didn't he?" said Shawn. "He wasn't able to talk at all until the baby was born, and he wrote on a tablet, 'His name is John.'"

"I'm glad that Mary believed the angel," said Jenna.

Then the family read all of chapter 2 of Luke, about Joseph and Mary traveling to Bethlehem for a census, and about the birth of Jesus and about Mary wrapping him in cloths and putting him in the manger.

"I knew that part," said Jenna. "Remember, I said he was put in a manger."

"That's right," said Drew. "She knew about that."

"But I didn't know that Mary was a virgin and that the baby Jesus was God's own son. Now I know that, but I don't understand it."

"Somehow, the Holy Spirit took care of that," said Cheryl, "but probably no one understands it."

Then the family finished chapter 2, reading about the angels appearing to the shepherds, the shepherds hurrying to see the baby, and about Mary and Joseph taking the baby to the temple. They read about the two people who recognized Jesus as the Messiah because the Holy Spirit had revealed it to them.

"What amazes me," said Richie, "is that with so many events about Jesus' birth and life that were prophesied, why weren't there more than two people who recognized Jesus as the Messiah they were expecting."

"Well, the wise men recognized his star and knew that he was to be the king of the Jews," said Shawn.

"Just like today," said Josh. "Jesus is coming back to get us soon, but most people aren't expecting him. I am expecting him though. It could be any day!"

"That is so true Josh and I'm happy you know that. It's getting kind of late for you boys," said Cheryl. "Maybe you should go to bed."

"Can't we just read about Jesus going to the temple when he was a boy?" asked Will. "It's my favorite part."

So they read about the boy Jesus going to the temple and his parents frantically looking for him. They found him in the temple having discussions with the teachers and they were amazed and Mary treasured all these things in her heart.

"I love this story of Jesus," said Jenna. "Whatever happened to him? Did he really die, like the boys said?"

"Yes," said Richie. "He died on the cross for our sins, and when we believe on him, God forgives us of all our sins."

"I believe it," said Jenna.

"That's wonderful Jenna," said Susan. "Maybe she can get baptized tomorrow. Would they open the church up for us?"

"I think that can be arranged," said Richie. "Do you want to be baptized?"

"What does that mean, to be baptized?" asked Jenna.

"We have a place at church to do baptisms, but it can be done in any body of water," said Cheryl. "First they ask you to repeat that you believe that Jesus is the Christ, the Son of God and that you accept him as your savior. Then someone helps you go down under the water and lifts you back up."

"I could baptize her, Mom and Dad. Could I do it?" asked Shawn.

Richie and Cheryl were really surprised that Shawn would want to do that at his young age, but Susan and Jenna both seemed good with it, so they agreed.

"Well I'll make a call and set up Jenna's baptism, and then I want to get to bed," said Richie. "I'm exhausted."

"I have some work to do for tomorrow," said Cheryl. "Jenna's other grandparents are coming for Thanksgiving."

"Uncle Jack and Aunt Karen are coming aren't they?" asked Susan. "I can't wait to play with our cute little girl cousins."

"Of course they'll be here," said Cheryl. "They wouldn't miss meeting Jenna."

Chapter 11

On Thanksgiving Day the whole family went to the church to baptize Jenna. Richie called the grandparents Fred and Evelyn to tell them what they were going to do, and the grandparents insisted on going too. So they all went to the church, and there were lots of their church friends there, including the preacher and his family and the youth minister and his family. Shawn did a fine job of baptizing Jenna, and everyone hugged her and welcomed her into the church.

Walking to their cars after the baptism, Grandma Evelyn said to Cheryl, "I think I told you that Harold's parents are coming to Thanksgiving dinner because of Jenna, but did I tell you that Harold's two brothers are coming too?"

"No," answered Cheryl. "If I remember right from Cynthia's wedding, they were just as arrogant and rude as Harold."

"That was my impression too," said Evelyn. "Well, they never got married, so since their parents are coming here for the meal, they want to come too."

"This might be the shortest Thanksgiving meal we ever had," said Cheryl. "If they get obnoxious, we'll just walk across the driveway, go in and take a nap, and then come back when they've all gone home."

"Thanks a lot!" said Evelyn.

Fred and Evelyn barely got in the door and the Ashcrafts arrived. The Ashcraft brothers lived in Cleveland and worked as managers in a casino. They all sat down and got comfortable, but when they discovered that the Jones family had no alcohol in the house, the two brothers left to go find a store of some kind that was open on the holiday and that sold bottles of booze. Harold's parents didn't go with them, and they didn't offer to help prepare the meal. That was fine with Evelyn, since she just about had the food ready. Then Jack and Karen and the three little girls arrived. The little girls went with Susan and Jenna to play with Grandma's toys and Jack and Karen set up the extra tables. Before long, they had the tables set for 19, with tablecloths, and all the plates and everything.

Soon Royal and Jackson, Harold's brothers, came back and they were cussing and complaining about the poor selection of alcohol in this God-forsaken area. Their pant legs and shoes and socks were wet from sloshing through the roads and walkways to get into the few stores they found that were open.

Richie, Cheryl, and all the kids came in with soft drinks, coffee, fruit salad, and many other things. And Fred and Evelyn were carrying all the rest of the food into the dining area. They all sat down and Fred said the prayer. This time Jenna bowed her head and closed her eyes and prayed with all her heart. She was brimming over with thankfulness.

Harold's parents were very grateful for their meal, but the Ashcraft brothers gobbled down their food, slipped into the kitchen and found and ate some pie, and then told their parents that it was time to go home.

"Oh no boys," said Helen their mother, "I haven't had a chance to visit with my dear granddaughter. And you two boys barely know your only niece."

"But we're cold, because our socks are wet!"

"Then you boys go in there by that fireplace, and warm your feet and dry your pants, while we sit in here and get to know our granddaughter," said their mom.

Grandma Evelyn stood up and began clearing the table and taking orders for pie. "Jenna, tell your Grandma Helen what you did this morning," she said.

"We went to the church and I got baptized!" said Jenna.

"That's nice dear," said Helen. "I wonder what your parents will have to say about that."

Jenna looked annoyed and said, "I'm not going back with them so I don't have to worry about that."

Cheryl looked pretty annoyed too. "It's more important that Jenna does what God says to do! We are so proud of her coming to faith in Jesus already," said Cheryl.

"Yes, that is nice," said Helen. "What are you going to do with your life now Jenna? Are you thinking about college?"

"Well, I would like to actually get my driver's license, and go to school with Susan and Josh, and go to youth group at church. Susan says it's so much fun," said Jenna.

"Maybe Jenna can go to a nice private college, so she can meet a future doctor or lawyer," said Grandma Helen. "She has to think of her future."

"Father is a lawyer Grammy, and I don't want to marry anyone like him!"

Grandma Evelyn spoke up about this subject. "After Cynthia married Harold, I wasn't going to let that happen to Cheryl or Jack. Oh no offence, Helen. Let's just say that Harold and Cynthia didn't bring out the best in each other."

"You can say that again," said Fred. "We went straight to our friends Vivian and Ralph for our matchmaking plan, didn't we Evelyn?"

"Yes," said Evelyn. "She had six children and she was determined they were all going to marry wisely."

"Tell them how they did it Evelyn," said Fred.

"It was very important to them that all of their children marry, not only a Christian, but also someone who goes to the same kind of church," said Evelyn. "She wasn't saying that they were better than other Christians. She just wanted her family to have the same beliefs and maybe go to the same Christian colleges or the same church camps or the North American Christian Convention. So when their oldest son was graduating from an art college in December, Vivian asked him how he would like to go to Kentucky Christian College for one semester, take some Bible classes, and find a wife. He said, 'OK.'"

Evelyn continued, "Micah was accepted at Kentucky Christian and began classes. He had a nice roommate. He called home every Thursday night to tell them how things were going. Each week he would discuss the Bible classes he was taking. Then he would tell about his progress finding a nice girl. Sometimes he would be interested in a certain girl, and the following week, he would say she wasn't right. When it was getting late in the semester, they decided that he should just stop worrying about finding the right girl and just have a good time."

"The last couple of weeks, four girls began including Micah in their activities. They were having a lot of fun together and even took him caving," said Evelyn. "Micah's friends would ask him if he liked one girl more than the others and he would usually deny it. But then his roommate said, 'He likes the redhead!' He was right."

"Micah and Bethany began dating at the end of that spring semester. He made many trips to Kentucky to visit her and her family," said Evelyn. "A year later, he proposed, and a year after that, they were married."

"So when their second son graduated from the same art college, Vivian mentioned that they couldn't afford to send him to Kentucky Christian to meet a nice Christian girl. He assured them that he would meet a nice girl at church. That's exactly what happened. So not only did Vivian and her husband get a good Christian daughter-in-law, but they also got grandparents for their future grandchildren, who go to their church," Evelyn said.

"That effort worked out for them with all of their children, but one. And they are still hopeful that he will find the right girl. Not only did they have wonderful Christian sons-and daughters-in-law, but their grandchildren all had two sets of Christian grandparents. So knowing about all of this from Vivian," said Evelyn, "Fred and I were determined not to lose any more of our children to a faithless life and a marriage."

Fred continued, "So when Cheryl graduated from high school, she was considering attending a party school with her girlfriends."

"Maybe I could have handled it, Dad," said Cheryl. "I would have searched for a campus fellowship."

"We were determined not to take a chance," said Fred. "So we told Cheryl she had to attend a Christian college for at least two years. She met Richie, a business major, and the rest is history. And the best result of all is those five Christian grandchildren."

"Six now, counting Jenna," said Susan.

"Hey, what about me?" said Jack. "You didn't have to make me go to a Christian college."

"We were very proud of you Jack," said Fred. "You wanted to be a preacher since you were about twelve."

"We're very thankful to God for our wonderful family," said Evelyn. "We made some good decisions, but we know God made our hopes and prayers come true."

Royal and Jackson, the Ashcraft boys, men really, came and joined the family, after a nice nap in front of the fireplace. "Can we go home now?" asked Royal. "Did you get enough time with your little granddaughter Mother?"

Suddenly there was a loud sound like thunder, and everyone there disappeared except for the Ashcraft family.

Chapter 12

"What just happened?" asked John Ashcraft. "Did I have a seizure or something? Where did everybody go?"

Helen answered, "No. We didn't go to sleep or anything. They just all disappeared right in front of us. I wouldn't believe it if I didn't see it."

"I feel creeped out," said Jackson. "Can we just go home and forget this happened? And I don't want to get blamed for missing people."

"Should we lock the doors on our way out?" asked Royal.

"Let's look around first," said Helen. "There might be some straggling kids around here. Remember there were a bunch of kids? And where is our Jenna?"

"Can we go home Dad?" asked Jackson. "And can I stay all night at your place tonight? I'm really freaked out and I can't go back to my apartment."

"That sounds good to me," said Royal. "I'll stay there too."

The Ashcrafts looked around, found their coats, and locked the doors on their way out. They went home, changed their clothes, and sat down together in front of the TV.

"Good evening. This is Jennifer Winter."

"And I'm Ben Clearwater. And this is the Six O'clock Evening News."

"Today, people from all over the world disappeared at 3:53 pm Eastern Standard Time. It's been a little over two hours since the chaos happened, everything from accidents caused by drivers and pilots disappearing, to train wrecks and robberies." The station showed scenes from around the state and a few from around the world. "Here in the states, many people had just finished their Thanksgiving dinners and others were just about to begin theirs." said Ben. "Jennifer, did you know any of the people who disappeared?"

"Well, my parents said they went to my Grandparents' house for Thanksgiving dinner, and the food was cooking, but no one was home. My grandparents could be at the hospital or someplace. We just don't know where they are."

"I'm sorry Jennifer. I'm sure they will turn up," said Ben.

"Well, their two dogs and the cat were all still there," said Jennifer. "But in other houses where people disappeared, we implore our viewers to take over the care of their pets. And please, peek in every vehicle to make sure there's not a precious dog left behind."

"So did your parents take your grandparents' pets home with them?" asked Ben.

"No, but they will check on them in the morning, and hopefully Grandma and Grandpa will be back."

"Now we turn to Ed Newsome for the weather," said Ben. "Ed!"

"First of all," said Ed, "I will try to answer the question about today's loud thunder boom. It was very unusual considering the temperatures were in the single digits and there was a lack of cloud cover. We don't usually hear thunder this time of year. But a thunder-like boom was heard in many places, so there has to be another explanation. Our best scientists are meeting together to figure it out, and when they do, they will let us know. And now for this week's forecast."

"That's it?" said Helen Ashcraft. "Those people on the news act as if the disappearances are no big deal! We just lost a whole houseful of friends and relatives in one sudden moment, right in front of our eyes! And where is my granddaughter? I just got her and now she's gone!"

"And did you notice, they didn't mention that the thunder boom happened at the same time as the disappearances?" said John Ashcraft. "Don't they get it?"

"I'm so creeped out, I don't think I'll ever sleep again," said Royal Ashcraft. "I've been talking to my drinking buddies, and some had it worse than we did."

"Worse than seeing fifteen people disappear off the face of the earth?" asked his dad.

"Yes," said Royal. "My friend Jerry has this cool sister Jazmin. She was on her way to her parents' house for Thanksgiving dinner, and her car was slammed into by a semi that lost the driver. Now she's in Aultman Hospital on life support and Jerry's family is devastated."

"Remember our drive home from the Jones's house?" asked Jackson. "There was a car with a telephone pole on top of it and another that obviously crashed into a Dairy Queen. I guess they lost their drivers. The newscasters act as if a pet left alone is the worst part of the day."

"I wonder how Harold and Cynthia are going to feel when they find out that Jenna is gone, really gone," said Helen.

"Maybe they disappeared too," suggested Royal.

"No," said his dad. "Don't you notice anything special about Evelyn and Fred Jones and all their family?"

"Not really," said Royal.

"Yes," said Jackson. "They were all really religious."

"That's true," said Helen. "You boys were in the other room when Fred and Evelyn told how they wanted their children and grandchildren to only marry Christians."

"Yes," said John. "They made sure their kids went where they married Christians.

"The point that your dad is making," said Helen, "is that their family was special. You know, really nice and God-fearing. When Jenna showed up last week they didn't have to tell us that she was there, but they knew it would mean so much to me."

"They even went to their church on Thanksgiving morning," said John. "They baptized Jenna, and she said she didn't care what Harold and Cynthia will think about it. Did you notice the change in her, Helen, in just a few days being with the Jones family?"

"I noticed," said Helen. And Helen just began sobbing.

"What's wrong, Mom?" asked Jackson.

"I don't know," said Helen. "Everything. I have a very bad feeling about all this."

"I think we have no idea about the fallout of these people disappearing," said John. "And I'm not talking about a bunch of cars crashing. Did you hear on the news that people are missing all over the world?"

"Dad, did people ever disappear before? What could cause such an event?" asked Royal.

"I don't know, and I don't know who to ask," said John.

"Fred and Evelyn would turn to the Bible for answers," said Helen. "I don't know if we even have one."

"I google most of my questions," said Jackson. "Maybe I'll try it."

"Since this never happened before, I doubt if you'll find any answers there," said John.

"According to this article, the event has been predicted in the Bible in several places," said Jackson. "It's called the Rapture, although it says the Bible doesn't call it that."

"Well I don't want to think about it or anything else," said Helen. "I'm going to bed."

"It's only 7:30," said John. "Let's watch a game or something."

"OK," said Helen. "That does sound soothing. Something normal to watch."

Royal tuned in to the Dallas Cowboys game against the Buffalo Bills. "I don't believe it," Royal said. "The words going across the bottom of the screen said that five players on the Cowboys team seem to be missing and their families don't know where they are."

"Well aren't they going to play anyway?" asked Jackson.

"It's not likely," said John. "They look like they don't know what they're going to do. The words going across the bottom say that they will have a news conference soon."

"Let's look for another game," suggested Royal. "I could use a good game about now." So Royal found another station with a football game going on. The announcer was explaining that on the New Orleans Saints team the quarterback didn't show up and no one knows where he is, and two other players were missing family members and were too distraught to play. Other team players were happy to fill in.

So the Ashcraft family watched a good football game and felt a little better about things.

Chapter 13

John and Helen Ashcraft just couldn't shake the thought of that whole family disappearing. They were nervous and nauseous. Neither John, nor Helen got any sleep the night before, and now they couldn't eat. John came into the room and said that he looked all over the house and couldn't find one Bible.

"So you think that maybe we can find some answers in the Bible about what happened to everyone who disappeared?" asked Helen.

"I just don't know where else to look," said John.

"Well let's go to Walmart and buy a Bible," said Helen. "I want to find out what happened to my girl Jenna."

So John and Helen Ashcraft went to Walmart and walked straight to the book section. Helen pointed to a clerk wearing a name tag.

"Excuse me Miss," said John. "We are looking for a Bible."

"That's interesting," said the clerk. "You are the third one to ask me for a Bible today." She walked over to the displays that held Bibles. "The Bibles are over here. What version do you want and what color?"

They had no idea about what version.

"My parents always encourage us to read the New International Version," said the clerk. "But we sell plenty of these other versions too."

"I'll take this one then," said John Ashcraft." He chose a navy blue copy of the New International Bible."

"I want one too," said Helen. She chose a red Bible that was the same size and version as John's.

John and Helen walked into their home, all ready to read their new Bible, and the phone was ringing.

"Let the machine pick it up," said John.

"No, but I promise not to talk long," said Helen. "Hello." Helen stood there, with the phone to her ear, but she seemed to be speechless.

"Who is it Helen," asked John. She looked at John, but didn't say anything. She handed him the phone.

"Hello, who am I speaking to?" asked John.

"This is your son Harold."

John looked at Helen and said, "He says it's Harold. Helen, why would he be calling?"

"Dad, I'm here with Cynthia, and we have a question for you. Have you seen our daughter Jenna?" asked Harold.

"Why would you ask me about your daughter?" asked John. "You never even told us that you have a daughter."

"Our neighbor girl and her mother came over when we got home from our trip," said Harold. "She said that Jenna ran away while we were gone and that she went to Ohio. Cynthia has been trying and trying to reach her parents, but they just don't answer the phone. So we thought we would call you." Helen was standing close and heard what Harold said.

"Oh John, you need to tell him what happened," said Helen.

"I know. Harold, Jenna did come to Ohio. Fred and Evelyn called us and invited us to come and meet Jenna last Sunday. We went and met her. And then they invited us to Thanksgiving Dinner, and Helen and I and Royal and Jackson all went and had dinner with them."

"Is she there? Can we talk to her?" asked Harold.

John was quiet for a moment. "Do you want me to tell him John?" John handed the phone to Helen.

"I'm sorry to tell you this Harold, but all of Fred and Evelyn's family, including Jenna, disappeared right in front of our eyes," said Helen. "We haven't gotten over the shock of it yet. Royal and Jackson also witnessed it and I guess they haven't slept since."

Harold was silent for a while. Finally he asked, "Why would they disappear? Where would they go? Do you think it's permanent?"

"We just don't know yet, but we are doing some research," said Helen. "We will let you know if we find out anything."

"We haven't talked about it yet, but we are supposed to go back to work tomorrow," said Harold. "Let me know if Jenna turns up."

"We don't even have your phone number, Harold," said Helen. "We haven't heard from you in years." Harold gave his parents their phone numbers and hung up.

"You know, Helen," said John. "I don't feel confident to just start reading the Bible. I wonder if Fred and Evelyn have any books about the disappearances. If we could find one, we could use our Bibles better. We would know where to look."

"We locked up their house," said Helen. "And I didn't think to take a key so we can get back in. Did you get one?"

"No, I didn't, but do you know what I just thought of?" asked John. "Their daughter Cheryl and her family were at Fred and Evelyn's house when they disappeared. They lived next door. Maybe they left their house unlocked. Let's get over there and see if their back door is unlocked."

"Oh I don't know John," said Helen. "I felt so creepy in their house after they disappeared. I'm not sure I want to go anywhere near there."

"Well, I'm going," said John. "Are you coming with me? We might not be able to get inside anyway."

"OK, I'm coming," said Helen. They got in the car and drove over to the house next door to Fred and Evelyn's house.

John and Helen walked to the door near the garage of the home of Cheryl Workman, the daughter of Fred and Evelyn. They tried the door and it opened right up. But when they went in, the house was not empty like they expected!

In the kitchen, John and Helen found two young men, helping themselves to food.

"Who are you?" asked John Ashcraft.

"We are neighbors from down the street and we just stopped in to check on the pets," said the first guy.

"So you decided to have a little snack," said John. "And did you find any pets in the house?"

"Uh, not yet," answered the other guy.

"Go on and get out of here before we call the police," said John.

The two guys grabbed their coats and the food they were eating and ran out the door.

"Wow," said Helen. "I was shaking all over. How did you know they don't have any pets?"

"Just a lucky guess," answered John as he locked the door. "Let's make sure the other door is locked as well."

John and Helen didn't exactly know what they were looking for. They walked in a room that looked like an office or a library. One book on a desk was called Living on Borrowed Time: The Imminent Return of Jesus, by David Reagan. Helen picked it up and put it in her huge purse. Harold gave her a funny look.

"What?" asked Helen. "They don't need it."

Then John saw a book out on another desk in the room called The Book of Signs: 31 Undeniable Prophesies of the Apocalypse, by David Jeremiah. "I'm taking this book," said John. "And you're right! They don't need these books now."

"Let's lock up the house, but this time we can take a key, just in case Harold and Cynthia want to stay at Cheryl's house if they come up here," said Helen.

"That's a very good idea Helen," said John. "We sure don't want them at our house."

John and Helen looked around the house before they left, just to make sure there weren't any pets. They went into Susan's bedroom while they were upstairs.

"Oh look John," said Helen. "This is the outfit that Jenna wore on that Sunday we met her. This must be her Bible. Inside the cover was a note to Jenna from her Grandpa Fred, expressing his love for her and his hope that she will become a Christian. There was a cell phone on the bed and Helen grabbed it and put it in her purse.

John and Helen finished looking around and didn't find any pets in the house. They left a few lights on so people will think someone is home. It only took a minute to figure out which keys locked up the place, so they took off for their home.

Chapter 14

Megan, Jenna's best friend, had been fuming since she and her parents went next door to tell Jenna's parents about Jenna running away. Jenna's parents didn't even thank them. In fact, they didn't seem to care, and they shut the door in their faces. Megan's parents told her to forget them. They weren't worth it.

Megan's phone rang and it was from Jenna. "Jenna! I have been so worried about you. Why didn't you call me back sooner?" asked Megan.

"I'm sorry Dear, but this isn't Jenna. I'm her grandmother," said Helen.

"I don't understand," said Megan.

"I'm Harold's mother," said Helen. "Yesterday, Harold called us, asking to talk to Jenna."

"Did he talk to her?" asked Megan.

"It wasn't possible," said Helen. "Jenna and the whole family disappeared right in front of our eyes; her other grandparents, all of their kids, except Cynthia (Jenna's mother), and all of their grandchildren."

"Are you saying that Jenna disappeared?" asked Megan.

"I'm afraid she did. We were getting ready to go home after our Thanksgiving Dinner. We heard this loud sound, like thunder. And suddenly everyone disappeared, fifteen of them. They were right there, and then they were gone," said Helen. "My husband and our two sons also witnessed it. As far as I know, there's never been anything like this."

"Why would Jenna disappear?" asked Megan. "I just don't get it."

"My husband and I think the answers might be found in the Bible," said Helen. "In fact, we went out and we each bought a Bible. Our son looked online someplace and it said that it is called the rapture, and it was predicted several places in the Bible. As soon as I get off the phone, I'm going to start reading it."

"Jenna never read the Bible, as far as I know," said Megan.

"Oh, those other grandparents of hers got her reading the Bible. She even got baptized on Thanksgiving morning," said Helen. "That's what the family all had in common. They were all into the Bible. So we are going to read the Bible until we figure out where they all went, and why."

"Maybe I'll get a Bible too," said Megan."

"Good for you," said Helen.

"Thanks for letting me know about Jenna," said Megan. "Goodbye."

———

Later that evening, Megan's family sat down to eat their dinner. Earlier, Megan had told her parents that Jenna and her whole family in Ohio had disappeared.

"Are you alright, Megan?" asked her mom. "You seem very quiet tonight."

"To tell the truth, I'm pretty messed up since I heard about Jenna," said Megan.

"You heard about the disappearances right after they happened. We sat here and watched the news together. You didn't seem upset at all," said Megan's dad.

"It didn't mean anything to me then," said Megan. "This is Jenna, my best friend. Where is she? She has to be someplace? Am I next? Will I just go away too, and you won't know where I went?"

"Stop it Megan! You're scaring me," said Megan's little sister Manda.

"What did Harold's mother tell you that has you so upset?" asked her mother.

"She said they were at their Thanksgiving dinner and they were talking. Suddenly there was a loud sound like thunder, and poof, they all disappeared. I think she said there were fifteen people there who disappeared. Everyone disappeared except Harold's mother and father and two brothers."

"Did they tell anyone?" asked Megan's dad.

"She told me," said Megan.

"They are probably upset too," said Megan's mom.

"They went out and bought Bibles," said Megan. "She said they think that is the only place to find out what happened. She said the Bible has many places that predict a disappearance like this."

Megan's parents looked at each other. Her father asked, "Do we have a Bible?"

"I have my mom's old Bible upstairs," said Megan's mother.

"My friend at work has the Bible on his phone. Now that I think about it, he didn't come to work this week. The boss told us that he didn't even call off, and that's just not like him," said Megan's Dad. "I wonder if he disappeared." He pulled his phone out of his pocket and called his friend. It rang and rang, but nobody answered. Megan's dad left a short message, but he had a feeling that his friend won't call back.

Megan's family moved into the family room and turned on the news, in hopes of hearing something about the disappearances. They listened intently and heard nothing about it.

"Can you believe it?" asked Mom. "It's like nothing happened. It's only been three or four days since the disappearances, and they didn't mention the event at all!"

"Even when the disappearances just happened, the news people acted as if it wasn't a big deal," said Megan's dad. "You know, tomorrow, if Andy doesn't show up for work, I'm going over to his house on my way home."

"If he's not there, maybe some of his family will be around," said Megan. "Dad, can I buy a Bible tomorrow after school?"

"I heard that Christian bookstore at the Strip Mall didn't open after Thanksgiving," said Megan's mom. "Maybe the owner wasn't around anymore to open it."

"I guess I can't buy a Bible there," said Megan.

"I'll take you to Target after school," said Mom. "I want to get one too."

"Are we going to put up some Christmas lights?" asked Manda. "The Reynolds across the street put theirs up."

The parents promised to put up the lights very soon. Since it was a school night, they tucked Manda and spent some time with Megan, trying to comfort her after the shock of losing her best friend.

Harold and Cynthia, next door, were fretting about many things.

"Oh Harold," said Cynthia. "I was the worst mother in the world. I'm sure no one was a worse mother than me. I was like that movie Mommy Dearest!

"I was terrible to her too. I know Jenna's gone, but I feel like we should go to Canton and talk to the family members who were with her," said Harold.

"What about your work?" asked Cynthia. "You just got back from vacation. Don't we need the money?

"Let's pack up the car in the morning and head for Ohio. We can stay with mom and dad in my old room," suggested Harold. "How is your work load?"

My job isn't real demanding," said Cynthia, "but I just lost some people that I always depend on. I suppose they disappeared."

"Maybe you can handle everything from your phone," said Harold. "No one needs to know you are out of state."

"Oh I don't know Harold. Your parents! They might not want to see us," said Cynthia. "And I don't blame them."

"It's too late to make amends with your family," said Harold. "But I still have time. And I want to hear about their visit with Jenna."

"I was really nasty to your mother," said Cynthia. "I don't think she will want to see me again."

"I want you to make up with Mother too," said Harold.

"Let me sleep on it Harold. I really need a drink, or maybe several drinks," said Cynthia. "This makes me really nervous."

"It will be alright Dearest," said Harold. "I'm going upstairs to bed, but first I'm going to pack my bag!" Cynthia went in the other room and started drinking.

Chapter 15

Everyone in the Ashcraft household, except Royal, who went to a bar, sat in their living room. Earlier, Helen had told her son Jackson about the book she brought home from Richie and Cheryl's house called <u>Living on Borrowed Time</u> and Jackson took it and couldn't put it down. "Jackson, are you about finished with that book I loaned you from Cheryl's house?" asked Helen. "I would like to read it."

"No Mom," said Jackson. "I'm intrigued. And I downloaded a Bible onto my phone and I'm checking out everything it says."

"What do you mean, you're checking it out?" asked Helen.

"Well this book, <u>Living on Borrowed Time</u>, was telling us to take the common sense meaning when reading prophesy in the Bible. The example was found in Zechariah 9:9. It read, 'Rejoice greatly, Daughter Zion! Shout, Daughter Jerusalem! See, your king comes to you, righteous and victorious, lowly and riding on a donkey, on a colt, the foal of a donkey.' This verse was talking about Jesus, before he was even born. Now, we can turn to any of the four Gospels. The Gospels, Mom and Dad, are Matthew, Mark, Luke, and John, the first four books of the New Testament. Oh I have learned so much in just one day!" said Jackson.

"So when did Jesus ride a donkey?" asked Helen.

"Look here in the book of John, chapter 21," said Jackson, "As they approached Jerusalem and came to Bethphage on the Mount of Olives, Jesus sent two disciples, saying to them, 'Go to the village ahead of you, and at once you will find a donkey tied there, with her colt by her.

Untie them and bring them to me. If anyone says anything to you, say that the Lord needs them, and he will send them right away.'"

"Do you even recognize this boy of ours Helen?" asked John.

"Next thing you know, he'll be going to church," said Helen.

"That's not possible," said Jackson.

"How do you know that?" asked John.

"Well, there might be churches, but if they were any good, their people are gone now," said Jackson.

"Who told you that?" asked Helen.

"I figured it out myself. Think about it," said Jackson. "Now listen to this, from the book of Matthew, chapter 24, verse 38,

'For in the days before the flood, people were eating and drinking, marrying and giving in marriage, up to the day Noah entered the ark; and they knew nothing about what would happen until the flood came and took them all away. That is how it will be at the coming of the Son of Man. Two men will be in the field; one will be taken and the other left. Two women will be grinding with a hand mill; one will be taken and the other left. Therefore keep watch, because you do not know on what day your Lord will come.'"

"Now we do know when the Lord came, don't we?" said John.

"Here in America, it was on Thanksgiving Day," said Jackson. "In most of the world, it was just a normal week day. And in some places, it was the middle of the night."

"So you think that's what happened Jackson?" asked Helen. "You think Jesus came and took Jenna and their whole family?"

"It looks that way," said Jackson. "Now I need to keep reading so we know where Jesus took them, and what is going to happen to those of us left behind."

"Well I'm exhausted," said Helen. "I'm going to bed."

"That sounds good to me," said John. "Good night Son. Let us know what you find out."

Just after John and Helen went upstairs, Royal came in the door.

"I thought you went home to your apartment," said Jackson.

"After what we witnessed the other day, I don't want to be alone," said Royal. "You can tease me if you want, but I'm freaking out."

"That's fine with me it you want to stay here with Mom and Dad," said Jackson. "I haven't gone back to my apartment yet either. My reasons are a little different than yours. Mom serves me breakfast, lunch, and dinner. They go to the store for groceries, and I'm free to sit here all day and study."

"What are you studying?" asked Royal.

"You're not going to believe it," said Jackson. "I'm studying the Bible, and I'm learning a lot."

"You are right," said Royal. "I don't believe it and I'm going to bed."

Jackson barely heard him, because he was fascinated with what he was reading now.

———

Harold and Cynthia got up the next morning and he was ready to pack up the car to go see his parents. Cynthia said she had a miserable headache, and Harold knew it was because of the alcohol she consumed before bedtime.

"Cynthia, do you remember those road trips we took, just you and me, when we would sneak off because we wanted to get away from Jenna? You know, when there was no school during the pandemic. Let's do that. I'll get you a hot chocolate and a sausage muffin and hash browns to eat on the way. And we'll stop at a Mexican restaurant for lunch."

Cynthia didn't feel hungry, but Harold made it sound comforting, and she really needed comfort. So Cynthia took a shower and quickly packed her suitcase. They headed for Canton, Ohio, and they were both worried that Harold's parents will hold a grudge because of their neglect.

———

Megan's father, Jimmy, went to visit his friend Andy after work. He rang the doorbell and banged on the door, but when he tried the door, it was unlocked. He walked in and yelled as he went into the house.

There was food sitting all over the dining room table and there were deserts in the kitchen. They apparently disappeared right in the middle of their Thanksgiving Dinner. He counted seven plates, so they must have had a set of grandparents there. He heard a meow and jumped.

"Well look at you. You scared me to death," said Jimmy, as he looked down at a beautiful, long haired calico cat. He decided to check the rest of the house. In an upstairs bedroom, Jimmy found an adorable little golden retriever puppy. "I guess I'm going to have to take you and kitty home with me. Now where do they keep the puppy chow and cat food?" In a pantry, Jimmy found not only cat and dog food, but clean bowls and a big container of kitty litter. He took those things to the car. When he came back, Jimmy looked for the litter box and when he found it, he decided to buy a new one rather than deal with that. After a lot of looking, he found a cat carrier and proceeded to put Kitty in it. Then he went on a search to find a box or tote to put the puppy in.

As Jimmy searched, he came across a desk that he figured was Andy's because it had a picture of his wife on it. Andy must have been looking at his Bible some time before dinner, because his reading glasses were right there, next to a notebook.

On the notebook next to the Bible was written something that got Jimmy's attention. *The rapture could take place any time now, because of two things prophesied in the Bible about the end times. First is that Israel will became a nation. This was prophesied in Ezekiel 37: 11-14. That happened on May 24, 1948. And according to Matthew 24:34 that generation will not pass away until all these things take place. Those people that were born in 1948 are 72 years old now. They will pass away relatively soon, well at least in the next 10 or 20 years.*

Andy also wrote, *Another reason I think the Lord will come for us soon is because on June 7th, 1967, the city of Jerusalem was won back to Israel. This was prophesied in Zechariah 8: 7 and 8, "This is what the Lord Almighty says: 'I will save my people from the countries of the east and the west. I will bring them back to live in Jerusalem; they will be my people, and I will be faithful and righteous to them as their God.'" I remember that President Trump moved the American Embassy to Jerusalem, a move that angered many people, but by doing so, he fulfilled prophesy.*

Then Andy wrote, *Call Bobby and warn him to reach out to the Lord in faith. Since he can't come to Thanksgiving dinner this year, I need to get ahold of him.*

He also wrote, *We need to be prepared because 1 Thessalonians 5:2 says, "for you know very well that the day of the Lord will come like a thief in the night."*

"*Or a thief in the daytime*," thought Jimmy. He decided to take the notebook and Andy's Bible with him. He managed to get the cat, puppy, notebook, and Bible into the car and go home.

Harold didn't give his parents much notice that they were coming, in fact, he called when they were only fifteen minutes away. John and Helen heard them pull up and went to the front door. They didn't rush out and hug them. Well, people seldom hug anymore since the great pandemic.

"Hello Mother. Hello Father," said Harold. "How are you?"

"Better than you two, I think," said John. "You both look like you were beat up."

"We were in that terrible earthquake in Italy," said Cynthia. "I have a broken arm and Harold had a concussion. And we both are bruised all over our bodies."

"We're alright," said Helen. "I'm really surprised you two came all this way. Jenna's gone. I doubt if she's coming back."

"Well," said Harold. "We are sorry for the way we treated you two all these years, and we just wanted to tell you."

"Really?" asked John. "You came to say you're sorry. You too Cynthia?"

"Yes, since my parents are gone, it's too late for us to make amends with them, but you two are still here," said Cynthia.

"Do you want to come in for a little while?" asked John.

"I ah, turned your room into a master suite, with a master bathroom, a walk-in closet, and a laundry room," said Helen.

"What about the boys' rooms?" asked Harold.

"The boys are both here," said John. "They were pretty upset after witnessing everybody disappearing, so they've been back in their rooms. Come on in and see them."

Harold and Cynthia walked in and saw Royal sleeping in the corner of the room. "Hello Royal," said Harold. Royal jumped and looked very distraught.

"What's going on?" asked Royal.

"It's Harold, Royal. He and Cynthia came up for a visit," said Helen.

"Where ya been all these years?" asked Royal. It was pretty obvious that he was drunk, and it really bothered Harold and Cynthia, because he looked just like Harold when he had had a few too many.

"Hi Harold, Cynthia," said Jackson. "If you came to pick up Jenna, you're too late."

"Mother told us about the family disappearing," said Harold. "So I guess we came to see all of you."

"That's nice," said Jackson, with a touch of sarcasm.

"Maybe we should go to a hotel," said Cynthia. "I didn't get much sleep last night."

"That's not necessary," said John. "We can let you into Cheryl's house. We have the key."

"Why would you have a key to Cheryl's house?" asked Cynthia.

"It's kind of a long story," said John. "How about we all meet at Poncho's tomorrow night for dinner? That used to be a favorite of yours, wasn't it Harold?"

"Yes," said Harold. "That sounds wonderful."

John grabbed the key off the wall, and gave it to Harold. "See you around six," said John.

"Six sounds fine," said Harold.

"Why should we stay at Cheryl's when Mom and Dad's place is right next door?" asked Cynthia.

"We locked up your parent's house, but we didn't think to take a key with us to get back in," said John. "Besides that, I don't think you want to deal with all of those dirty dishes. We left in quite a hurry.

"I saw Evelyn put the dishes to soak before we had our pie, so I'm sure the house is fine," said Helen. "Do you still have your key to your parents' house, Cynthia?"

"No," said Cynthia. "We'll stay at Cheryl's."

Before they walked out to the car, Harold said to his dad, "We can't get over all these mountains of snow."

"Didn't you hear about the Great Blizzard of 2020? It was unbelievable. Many people died."

"No," said Harold. "We were in Rome, where we witnessed the Great European Earthquake."

"This has been quite a year," said Helen. "The Great wildfires in California, the Great Worldwide Pandemic, the Great East Coast Hurricane, and the Great Blizzard. Oh, and not to leave you out, the Great European Earthquake."

"Oh my," said Jackson. "This was all prophesied too! God has been trying to wake us up and get us to turn from our sin. If we would have listened to him, we wouldn't be here now."

"Well, I'm glad we're still here," said Harold.

"You won't be glad for long," said Jackson. "We are all going to be very sorry we didn't listen to God."

"Jackson, come with us tomorrow to the restaurant and tell us all about it, although I'm not sure I want to know." said Helen. "Did you know, Harold that your brother Jackson is getting to be an expert on Bible prophecy?"

"That's interesting," said Harold.

So Harold and Cynthia went to Cheryl and Richie's house and took their bags inside.

———————

Harold and Cynthia got into their comfortable clothes and watched TV for a while. Harold went to the kitchen to look for a snack, and noticed the lights on next door, and someone walking around.

"Cynthia, someone is next door in your parents' house. Do you think they came back?" asked Harold.

"Turn out the lights!" said Cynthia. "Let's watch and see who is in there."

They stood there in the dark for a long time, and finally someone walked by the window. It was definitely a stranger.

"That should be my house," said Cynthia. "Call your dad and ask him what we should do."

Harold's dad told them that he heard on the news that a lot of people were moving into nicer houses and filing for squatters' rights. If there aren't any relatives alive, they can keep the place.

"Well they do have relatives alive, us! We get first dibs on that house. It's an amazing house," said Cynthia. "Should we call the police?"

"Let's just go next door and tell them it's your house," said Harold.

"But I'm in my pajamas, Harold," said Cynthia.

"And you look very cute in them Dearest," said Harold. "Let's go."

So Harold and Cynthia walked across the driveway and knocked on the backdoor.

A woman came to the door and looked out the window.

"Open up," said Harold very loudly.

The woman opened the door and said, "Can I help you folks?"

"What are you doing in my parent's house?" asked Cynthia in her mayor voice.

Harold and Cynthia walked in.

"I'm sorry," the intruder said. "During the blizzard, I stayed here with Fred and Evelyn and I noticed that it is a very nice house. I stayed in one of the bedrooms and I opened the window a little. I remembered it and thought we could come over and check on the family,"

"So you decided to just move in?" asked Harold.

"My name is Angie. A lot of people live in our tiny, little one-bathroom house. I just thought the family must have disappeared. Is Jenna still around? What about Shawn?"

Cynthia lost her edge at the thought of Jenna being who knows where. "No," Cynthia said. "She's gone. My whole family is gone."

"I'm so sorry," said Angie. "I still have my whole family, and I am very thankful for that. But do you need both houses? Is Cheryl and her whole family gone too?"

"Yes, they are all gone," said Cynthia. She looked at Harold because she was at a loss for words.

"Let's sleep on it Cynthia. We can discuss this later," said Harold.

"Thanks for letting us stay tonight at least. The children are already asleep," said Angie.

"We'll let you know what we intend to do," said Cynthia. "Good night."

Angie closed the door and looked at her husband, "I've been in both of these houses. Granted this house is a little fancier, but Cheryl's house has more bedrooms and bathrooms. I think, if they could have mercy on us, and let us stay in one or the other, we could be set for a very happy, comfortable life."

"That sounds good to me," said Ernie, Angie's husband. "Of course, they might kick us all out in the morning."

Chapter 16

Jimmy White, Megan's dad walked in the house from the garage carrying a puppy and a cat in a carrier. His wife Kara, looked annoyed, but the girls went crazy. Megan grabbed the puppy and sat on the floor and snuggled it and Manda opened the door of the carrier, pulled the cat out, and sat down by her sister.

"Can we keep them Dad, Please?" asked Manda.

"I thought maybe we should," said Jimmy, "since they don't have a family anymore."

Jimmy motioned for Kara, his wife, to go in the other room. "What do you think?" he asked. "I thought about calling home, but I had my hands full with the puppy."

"When you walked in with them, I wanted to tell you to turn right around and take them back," said Kara. "But did you see Megan's face? This is the happiest I've seen her since she found out about Jenna. This is just what she needed."

"It appears that Andy, his wife, his three kids, and maybe a couple grandparents all disappeared as well," said Jimmy. "Their place really needs cleaned up because of all that food sitting around."

"Maybe a relative or neighbor will come and check on them," said Kara. "Did you lock up the place?"

"I did," said Jimmy. "I walked right in because the door was unlocked, and luckily no one else noticed. But I locked up when I left."

"I guess we need to go to a pet store," said Kara.

"Yes, but just to get a litter box. They had everything else in the pantry, and I brought it with me," said Jimmy. "Andy knew the disappearances were going to happen soon. He had a Bible and some notes and I brought those things home too."

"How did he know?" asked Kara. "I thought no one knew when."

"He didn't know what year or month," said Jimmy. "He thought it would be in the next ten or twenty years. But I think he had a feeling that it was close."

———

John and Helen Ashcraft were discussing the recent events and they were feeling overwhelmed. The disappearance of fifteen people in their presence was something to get over. Then their two sons moved in with them, creating a lot more work and expense. And then Harold and Cynthia showed up at the door.

"Helen, do you think our life will ever be the same? I just don't know what to think about people disappearing? How can we go on as if that didn't happen?" asked John. "The news people seem to have forgotten already, and yet I heard that people are drinking more and there has been an increase in suicides already."

"I suppose some people lost a lot of loved ones, and couldn't imagine living without them," suggested Helen.

"I'm afraid to ask Jackson what he meant when he said that we will all be sorry that we are still here," said John.

"Jackson is obsessed," said Helen. "And this is just like him. Remember how he wanted to solve the Rubix cube, and he stayed up half the night for who knows how many days until he solved it. And then he was into juggling, and he spent days learning that. This is just another obsession."

"Oh no," said John. "This is different. You know Helen, my parents always took us to church and Sunday school. Once I was in high school, I thought it was boring, and I told them that I was not going to go after I graduated from high school. I never went back. But Mom told me she was praying for our family that we would all become Christians. When she was dying, she begged me to promise that we would at least go to church, but I wouldn't. She said that she would pray for our boys, and die believing we would all become Christians. That's what is going on with Jackson. It's the answer to my mom's prayers."

"Jackson said there aren't any churches anymore," said Helen.

Jackson walked in the door just in time to hear what Helen just said. "I said there probably aren't any good churches anymore," said Jackson. "I finally went to my apartment and got all of my stuff out and gave the keys back to the landlord. Luckily there's a waiting list and someone wants to move in in December, so I'm good. I left most of the stuff in my car, but I brought in some clean clothes, my laptop, and this, the Bible Grandma Ashcraft gave me. I forgot all about it."

"I was just discussing your grandma with your mom," said John. "Grandma wanted us all to become Christians. I just ignored it, even though it was her dying wish. I guess I just didn't want to change our lives. Well, at least I didn't lie to her. I didn't make her a promise that I had no intention of keeping."

"Well, I loved Grandma Ashcraft, and I miss her so much. I never once doubted that she loved me," said Jackson. "And I'm going to make her dying wish come true. I haven't figured it all out yet, but I'm going to become a Christian. I just wish so much that I would have done it sooner. Then I would be with her in heaven, and I would be safe."

"Don't you feel safe?" asked Helen.

"No Mom," Jackson said. "We are soon going into a terrible period of time called the tribulation. I'm not sure what all is going to happen, but it will be bad. You've heard jokes about 666 all your life, right? Well, whatever you do, don't let anybody put that number on your hand or your forehead. It's the devil's mark."

"So you think we're doomed, Jackson?" asked John. "Should we just kill ourselves and get it over with?"

"No," answered Jackson. "But I think it's going to be really bad for a while. We will probably all die. Chapter 6 of Revelation covers the seven seals and I'm guessing they are what happens in the beginning of the Tribulation, which might start any day now. I think there's going to be some kind of conqueror, and I hope he doesn't conquer America. Then there will be no peace on the earth and people are going to kill each other. That could be something like the riots we saw all over the world in June, July, and August."

Royal had slipped into the room and had been listening to everything. "I hope you're kidding about all that," said Royal.

"Royal, this is serious, and I think it's going to happen just as it says. The third seal sounds like inflation, where you have to work all day, just to buy some wheat. I think that's like buying flour. And then in the fourth seal, one fourth of us people on earth are going to die, and you aren't going to like this. They're going to die by the sword, famine, plague, and by wild beasts, and I think that means wild animals, don't you?"

Helen looked terrified, and said, "Oh no! I don't want to run from wild beasts. And I can't go through another coronavirus scare. Jackson, What can we do?"

"According to Acts 2, verse 38, we need to be baptized in the name of Jesus Christ for the forgiveness of our sins and the gift of the Holy Spirit," said Jackson. "I just hope there are others around who can support us and be with us."

"In other words, Jackson, what you want is a church, like Grandma Ashcraft begged us to go to," said John.

"Yes," said Jackson. "I think I always wanted that. I don't know why I didn't insist. As a child, I was jealous of my friends talking about going to youth group or church camp. When I was in college, I would hear about guys going to a campus fellowship, and it sounded so good. Why didn't I go with them? If I would have, I would probably be in heaven right now, with a new body, and with Jenna, and the whole Jones family, and with Grandma and Grandpa Ashcraft!"

"I think I need a few drinks," said Royal.

"No, Royal," said Jackson. "You don't need a few drinks. You need God, and Jesus, and the Holy Spirit. Then you will feel the peace you are searching for in a bottle."

Royal looked really startled and didn't know what to think or what to say. He got up and said, "So those were the first four seals and there are three more. Do they all get worse after that?"

"Actually, I kind of like the fifth seal, because it is about people like us," said Jackson.

"Listen to this starting at Revelation, chapter 6, verse 9."

When he opened the fifth seal, I saw under the altar the souls of those who had been slain because of the word of God and the testimony they had maintained. They called out in a loud voice, "How long, Sovereign Lord, holy and true, until you judge the inhabitants of the earth and avenge our blood?" Then each of them was given a white robe, and they were told to wait a little longer, until the full number of their fellow servants, their brother and sisters, were killed just as they had been.

"So that was the fifth seal, and that is supposed to give me comfort?" said Royal. "I'm going to my room and take a long nap."

"I think I could use some time to myself as well," said Helen. She had tears running down her cheeks as she went off to her bedroom.

"I'm going out for a long walk, but I'm sure we'll discuss all of this tonight at Panchos, when we have dinner with Harold and Cynthia," said John. "Keep on studying Jackson."

"You know I will Dad," said Jackson.

Back in New Jersey at Megan's home, her dad Jimmy was studying the Bible and notes of his work friend Andy, who had disappeared along with his family. Something was bothering Jimmy about Andy, and it took a few days to realize what it was. Andy had written that he needed to call Bobby and encourage him to become a Christian. Jimmy realized that he should call Bobby and share with him about Andy's concern for him. Jimmy put his pen down and took off to Andy's house to look for his phone. He looked around the house and finally found a phone on the table, right next to a bowl of cranberry sauce. Jimmy looked for a purse, thinking that Andy's wife or a grandmother, probably left a phone there. Sure enough, he found a phone in a purse. Jimmy took both phones, locked the house and went home.

Later that evening, Jimmy found time to check out the phones. Luckily, Andy's phone wasn't locked. He looked at calls, and sure enough, there were 27 calls and messages from Bobby. He listened to a few of the messages, and Bobby sounded heart-broken, thinking that something horrible must have happened to Andy, and to their mom and dad. It was only 9:00 pm, so Jimmy decided to call Bobby.

"I know this can't be Andy, after all these days have gone by. So who is this?" asked Bobby.

"I'm Andy's work buddy, Jimmy," he answered. "Our boss was ready to fire Andy for not showing up for work, even though he's never been late. So I wondered if maybe he disappeared. I finally decided to go over to his house and sure enough, there were empty seats around a Thanksgiving dinner. I took home his Bible, his notebook, a cat, and a puppy. Then I went back and got his phone and a phone that was in a lady's purse, so I could let their loved ones know what I found there."

"Andy is my brother. If that was my mom's phone you found, it probably has about seventy-five calls and messages from me," said Bobby. "I really wanted to hear my mom's voice."

"I'm sorry I didn't think to call you sooner," said Jimmy.

"So you're pretty sure they disappeared?" asked Bobby

"It looks that way. Do you know if your parents were going to Andy's for Thanksgiving? There were seven seats there for Thanksgiving Dinner," said Jimmy. "I didn't clean up the food, thinking someone might want to see it to believe it."

"Yes," said Bobby. "My parents flew to New Jersey to spend time with his family. They were going to spend Christmas with us."

"Why do you think your brother's family and your parents disappeared, and you didn't?" asked Jimmy.

"I have no clue!" said Bobby. "I find it hard to believe that they are among those who disappeared. Do you have any ideas about that?"

"The whole reason that I went back to Andy's house to look for his phone was because of this note in his notebook," said Jimmy. "It was laying open next to his Bible and his glasses. This is what he wrote that might give you some insight. 'Call Bobby and warn him to reach out to the Lord in faith. Since he can't come to Thanksgiving dinner, I need to get ahold of him.'"

"Is that supposed to give me insight?" asked Bobby. "He's been after me to get more serious about church and God since we were teenagers. So what's new?"

"What's new is that Jesus came down and zapped your brother and his whole family and your parents, and took them up to heaven, along with other believers from the whole world. Now they are all up there with brand, new eternal bodies and are living in complete safety. And we are here, and we are about to endure the horrible seven year tribulation, and we probably won't even live through it," said Jimmy. Jimmy was startled to see Megan standing nearby, looking shocked. "Bobby, I'm going to have to call you back. I think my daughter needs to talk to me."

"Don't bother to call me back," said Bobby. "I've heard enough!" And he hung up.

Jimmy put the phone down, and held his arms out for Megan to come sit on his lap. She sat down and started sobbing.

"Ever since I heard about Jenna disappearing, I've had this sick feeling that things aren't ever going to be good again," said Megan. "I'm right, aren't I Dad?"

"Yes and no," said Jimmy. "I've been reading the notes made by my friend Andy, and looking up verses in the Bible. There will be seven years of dreadful things happening. But we need to turn our hearts to God. He will protect us, and even if we die, we will go to heaven and be with God and Jesus and Jenna and all of the Christians forever and ever."

"I don't want to die, Dad," said Megan. "I want to grow up."

"Well you're seventeen now, so you'll be twenty-four if you survive the next seven years," said Jimmy. "And we are going to study the Bible and figure out the right things to do. But let me read something to you from the Bible that is just about people like us, who missed out on the rapture."

So Jimmy read from Revelation 7:9, through the end of the chapter.

> After this I looked, and there before me was a great multitude
> that no one could count, from every nation, tribe, people,
> and language, standing before the throne and before the
> Lamb. They were wearing white robes and were holding palm
> branches in their hands. And they cried out in a loud voice:

"Salvation belongs to our God, who sits on the throne, and to the Lamb."

All the angels were standing around the throne and around the elders and the four living creatures. They fell down on their faces before the throne and worshiped God, saying: "Amen! Praise and glory and wisdom and thanks and honor and power and strength be to our God for ever and ever. Amen!"

Then one of the elders asked me, "These in white robes-who are they and where did they come from?"

I answered, "Sir you know." And he said, "These are they who have come out of the great tribulation; they have washed their robes and made them white in the blood of the Lamb. Therefore, "they are before the throne of God and serve him day and night in his temple; and he who sits on the throne will shelter them with his presence.

'Never again will they hunger; never again will they thirst. The sun will not beat down on them,' nor any scorching heat. For the Lamb at the center of the throne will be their shepherd; 'he will lead them to springs of living water,' 'And God will wipe away every tear from their eyes.'"

"So we might be hungry and thirsty and maybe even sunburned?" asked Megan.

"Even worse," said Jimmy. "We might get tortured. We might get our head chopped off."

"Dad, why are we in this mess?" asked Megan. "Didn't your friend tell you this was coming?"

"No he didn't. But he was a good friend," said Jimmy.

"What kind of friend was he, if he knew we were in danger, and didn't say anything?" asked Megan.

"Well, he probably didn't even know I wasn't a believer," said Jimmy. "I'm a pretty nice person. It's hard to tell. But I knew Andy was a believer. And I should have listened to my Aunt Josie. She witnessed to me a few times. I need to call her, but I bet she won't answer."

"Are you going to tell Mom and Manda?" asked Megan.

"Mom and I already talked about it, and we're planning to look for a church so we can tell someone that we believe and get baptized," said Jimmy. "But Manda doesn't need to know yet."

"I love you Dad," said Megan. "Thanks for telling me the truth."

"Well, you kind of forced it on me when you walked into the room," said Jimmy.

"You could have made up something," said Megan. "This way I can help figure things out."

Chapter 17

All of the Ashcraft family met at Panchos for dinner, and they were waiting outside for their table. John, Helen, and Royal looked terrible. Jackson looked all business as he carried in a Bible and a large binder. Harold and Cynthia looked pretty good and relaxed.

"Did you two have a good rest at Cheryl's house last night?" John asked Harold and Cynthia.

"As a matter of fact, we did," said Harold.

"Something wonderful happened," said Cynthia. "We found Cheryl and Richie's will. Of course, in case they died, they left everything to each other, and then to their children. But they had a special clause in their will, that if their family all disappeared in the rapture, the property was to go to me, since I am the only one in Cheryl and Richie's family who they expected to still be around."

"So are you two planning to stay here and live in Cheryl's house?" asked Helen.

"No," said Harold. "But we are thinking about staying here."

"Remember, Harold, that Mom and Dad turned your room into their laundry room and Master bathroom," said Royal. "And you can't have my room."

"We don't need your room, Royal. We actually have two houses here in town, not to mention our place in New Jersey. Someone was actually living next door in Fred and Evelyn's house, so we confronted them," said Harold. "Remember, I called you about it, Dad?"

"Yes, what happened?" asked John.

"We let them stay the night and went back this morning, and you'll never guess what we found," said Cynthia. "We found my parents' will too. My parents did the same thing as Cheryl," said Cynthia. "They left their house to me. It's really nice."

"So we're going to sell our place in New Jersey and live here," said Harold. "We had the squatters living in the parents' house move to Cheryl's for now and we moved into Fred and Evelyn's. We might charge them rent, or just have them take care of both houses, like shoveling the driveways and mowing the yard, stuff like that. Cynthia called and will quit her job, since she can't be the mayor if she lives in Ohio. But I can work from anyplace. So we will have it pretty nice and comfortable here."

"Is that what you think? Wait until you hear about the wild beasts and the plague that are coming," said Royal. "I'm afraid of dogs, so I will be terrified of wild beasts, and what if it's a famine? I hate to be hungry."

"What are you talking about?" asked Cynthia.

"Oh, Jackson has been doing some research into prophesy in the Bible," said John. "He has us all scared out of our minds."

"I didn't even get to the beheadings yet," said Jackson.

Just then the family was called to go to their table. Once seated, they all looked at Jackson, not sure if they wanted him to ruin their dinner.

"Please Jackson, let us at least order our food before you tell us about losing our heads," said Helen.

"Yes, let's order, and I'll tell you the bad news while they are cooking everything," said Jackson.

As soon as the drinks were served, the family began chatting.

"Tell me about the family staying in Cheryl's house," said John.

"Well, they could never afford a big house like that," said Cynthia. "Angie is a bus driver and her husband hasn't found a job since the pandemic. They have three children and two mothers, who are widows that live with them. They are moving into Cheryl and Richie's big house, and Angie's sister and two children will move in with them. So I guess, we are helping ten people."

"Are you going to charge them rent?" asked John.

"We are thinking about having them take care of their yard and ours," said Cynthia.

"I think you and Harold have changed," said John.

"I would like to think we have changed," said Harold. "While we were recovering from our broken bones and head wounds, we had plenty of time to reflect on our lives. We are very sorry for the way we treated you, Mom and Dad, not to mention our relationship with Jenna."

"We have lived very selfishly, and a lot of it was because of our dependency on alcohol and drugs, not that all of that is an excuse." said Cynthia.

"Yes, coming off of all that was difficult," said Harold, "especially because we were in so much pain. But because of the earthquake, they were short on supplies in Rome, and we couldn't get any pain killers. We arrived home clean, and realized we felt better than we had in a long time. Cynthia drank the night before we came here, and didn't feel good afterwards. Except for that, we don't have the ups and downs anymore. We are almost mellow. Right Dearest?"

"Well you're not going to be mellow when you are running from rhinos and tigers," said Royal.

"What on earth are you talking about?" asked Cynthia.

"He's talking about the Tribulation," said Jackson. "That is the seven years that follow the rapture."

"The very idea of that sends chills throughout my body. And, Jackson, what were you starting to tell us about getting beheaded?" asked Helen.

"I'm sure you have all heard of the antichrist," said Jackson. "Well, there is also a false prophet. And the false prophet will force the people to make an image, like an idol, of the antichrist. It's probably going to be really big. Anyone who won't worship the image will be killed. And people have to get the number 666 on their right hand or on their forehead, and if they don't get it, they can't buy or sell. And you know what that means, don't you?"

"I think I know," said Royal. "It means we can't eat, so we will die."

"That's right," said Jackson. "Now John, who wrote this book of Revelation, the last book of the Bible, said this in chapter 20, verse 4b."

And I saw the souls of those who had been beheaded because of their testimony about Jesus and because of the word of God. They had not worshiped the beast or its image and had not received its mark on their foreheads or their hands. They came to life and reigned with Christ a thousand years.

"I hope that's going to be all of us," said Royal. "Not the beheading part, of course, but that we are the ones who are God's people."

"Even to our death?" asked Jackson.

"Yes," said Royal. "And I hope I would be brave enough."

"Do you really believe all of this Jackson?" asked Harold. "What about you Mom and Dad?"

"I wouldn't have believed that people could just disappear right in front of my eyes," said Helen. "But they did. Poof and they were gone."

"That's right," said Jackson. "And it sounds like some people, like Cheryl and Richie and Fred and Evelyn believed the prophecies in the Bible and were prepared by putting it in their will. When did they write those wills by the way?"

"They were dated eight years ago," said Harold. "Richie and Cheryl's will included their twins, who were just babies at the time."

The Ashcraft family had no idea that people in the restaurant were listening in. But when

their food arrived, they noticed. Some people were even standing up and had moved closer so they could hear what they were saying.

"Can we help you?" asked Jackson.

"Well after you eat your meal, will you teach us more?" asked an older man.

A young couple was standing nearby and the man asked Jackson, "Would it be possible for you to come to our church and speak this Sunday? We could really use some help."

"Yes," answered Jackson. "I've been wanting a church to go to. I've never gone to one before."

"Thank you," answered the man. "I'll write down the information for you. This is definitely an answer to our prayers."

As Jackson and the family ate their meal, they noticed many in the restaurant were writing down something. Soon the young man came over and gave Jackson a sticky note with the church's name and address and the time 10:00 am. He said, "Several of these other families will be joining us this Sunday. We'll see you then." The man got Jackson's name and phone number and left.

Royal said, "You know Jackson. When all of the disappearances happened, and then when you started telling us about the future, I was freaking out. But now, I have a sense of peace about the whole thing. I used to be scared out of my mind, even earlier today, and now I feel almost brave. What could cause that?"

John Ashcraft answered. "This could be your grandmother's dying prayers coming true."

"Or it could be the work of the Holy Spirit," said Jackson.

"I'll go to church too," said Royal. "Maybe I can help in some way."

"You're pretty technical, Royal. We can make up the messages together, and maybe make a power point or something," said Jackson.

"What is the Holy Spirit?" asked John.

"I have a lot to learn, but I guess the Holy Spirit is a He, not it, and he's part of God; God the Father, God the Son, Jesus, and God the Spirit," said Jackson. "Mom and Dad, do you want to go to church Sunday and listen to me preach?"

"I guess we could give it a try," said Helen.

"Don't you guys get it?" asked Jackson. "What we do now will result in either everlasting life or eternal misery. Please Mom. I want you with me in heaven. You too Dad."

"Of course we'll go," said John. "I'm proud of you Jackson. And you're really coming along too, Royal."

"Thanks Dad," said Royal. "I'm still a little scared about wild beasts, though. Remember how I had nightmares for weeks after seeing that snapping turtle. And remember the Reynold's dog next door? I didn't go out to play for years. But except for that, I'm coming along."

"What do you say, Cynthia Dear?" asked Harold. "Should we go to that church to hear Jackson preach?"

Cynthia made a reluctant face. "I don't think so," said Cynthia. "I was never a fan of church."

"Oh come Dear," said Harold. "This is just Jackson, not some pressure preacher."

"Are you kidding? Didn't you hear his speech a few minutes ago?" asked Cynthia. "He was talking about eternal misery. I think I need a drink, Harold."

"No Cynthia," said Harold. "We've come so far. Let's don't go there again."

"Harold, let's go back to my parent's house. I need a rest, at least," said Cynthia.

"Of course we can," said Harold, "but remember, it's not your parent's house. It's our house now Dearest." They paid for their food and took off.

In New Jersey, Megan's family was reading through the book of Revelation in the Bible, and they weren't having much luck understanding it. And then Helen called Megan to see how she was getting along.

"Oh Mrs. Ashcraft," said Megan. "Terrible. We are not understanding the Bible at all.

Someone told my dad to read the last book in the Bible because that will explain what's going to happen next. And we are just lost."

"If you haven't read much of the Bible, you probably shouldn't start with Revelation," said Helen.

"Well where should we start?" asked Megan.

"First of all, you need to get to know Jesus," said Helen. "Turn to the New Testament and read Matthew, Mark, Luke, and John. I'll ask my son Jackson what to read after that. You can call me anytime you need to and I'll call you when I find a plan to read through the Bible."

Megan wrote down what Helen said, and then said to her, "Thank you so much Mrs. Ashcraft. We'll get busy reading those four books you suggested, and I'll talk to you about it later."

Chapter 18

Jackson and Royal worked better together than they ever did before. They met the nice man from Panchos who invited them to his church. His name was Alan, and Alan thought they should see the church and figure out how things worked. There was another guy there named Max, and he made a suggestion.

"I just had an idea, and I think it's a very good one," said Max. "During the pandemic, we couldn't attend church, so we did our services online. Do you remember that?"

"No, I don't remember that," said Jackson. "This will be my first time to attend a church."

Max looked really concerned, and looked at Alan and asked, "Don't you think he should listen to a few sermons before he preaches one? We could play reruns of Jared's sermons for months."

"Oh no," said Alan. "Jackson's a natural. He was just talking the other night at Taco Tuesdays, and the people in the restaurant were gathering all around him, including me."

"How do we know if he's going to be teaching the right doctrine, you know, what our church believes?" asked Max.

"A lot of good that doctrine did us," said Alan. "We're still here and our preacher didn't disappear, he was killed by a runaway car whose driver disappeared. He didn't tell us that we were in danger of missing out on the rapture. We didn't make it to heaven with some of our families. This guy, Jackson, gets it. He will tell us what's coming next. Right, Jackson?"

"I don't know if I'll be any good at this," said Jackson. "Maybe he's right. I never set foot in church before. What do I know about it?"

"Jackson, you've got this," said Royal. "Remember what you told me just yesterday from Ephesians 2:10. 'For we are God's handiwork, created in Christ Jesus to do good works, which God prepared in advance for us to do.' And I think this is our job to do!"

"Thank you Royal," said Jackson. "I needed that." So Jackson and Royal studied the church sanctuary, from the cameras and screens, to the baptistry and pulpit.

Jackson and Royal figured out how to put the scriptures up on the screens.

"What about the Lord's supper," asked Jackson. "This will be our first time to take it."

"Oh that won't be necessary," said Max. "We don't do communion every week. It's more like every other month."

"Really?" asked Jackson. "I was just reading that we are supposed to take it whenever we meet together."

"Not necessary," said Max.

"We will have the Lord's Supper," said Jackson, "or we will find another church to meet in. And I noticed the baptistry doesn't have water in it. Who is in charge of filling it?"

"I think we have deacons who take care of things like that," said Alan.

"I guess Royal and I can learn how to prepare the communion and how to fill the baptistry with water," said Jackson.

"That won't be necessary," said Alan. "I'll be happy to take care of those things. And I will stand at the door as people enter, because I'm a greeter! You just take care of the message! Oh, and what would you like me to put on the message screen outside?"

Jackson thought a minute and then said, "Did you miss the Rapture? Eternal life is still possible! Sunday 10 am!"

————————

Sunday arrived and Jackson and Royal went to the church and set up early.

"You know, Royal, I'm a little nervous," said Jackson. "I never preached before, and I want to do a really good job."

"Just pretend we're back in Panchos, and you are teaching the Ashcraft family," said Royal.

"Good idea. I really hope the family shows up this morning," said Jackson.

The boys were well prepared when people started arriving, with all of the scripture verses loaded in for Royal to put on the screens at just the right time. They joined Alan at the door and met people as they came in, including John and Helen and Harold. Cynthia had a headache and was still asleep when Harold left.

Almost every seat was taken by 10 am, so Jackson went to the pulpit and Royal went to the media center. Jackson began his sermon by describing his life.

Jackson began, "As long as I can remember, even as a little boy, I was looking for something. But nothing was ever as exciting as I hoped. Fireworks, Disney World, the zoo, a swim park, a skate park, a tour of the White House or the Space Center. You can ask Mom and Dad. I was always disappointed. I wanted to do something with meaning."

"After my family and I witnessed 15 people disappearing right in front of our eyes on Thanksgiving Day, my life changed. First, I had the biggest mystery of my life to solve. The first thing I did was Google a question like, 'Will people on earth disappear?' Do you realize that many people knew that people were going to disappear? That's because it is prophesied in the Bible. While I'm on the subject of prophesy, there were many prophesies about the birth of Jesus in the Old Testament that were fulfilled at his birth and not that many people were expecting him. They weren't paying attention. I'll name a couple."

"In Isaiah, chapter 7, verse 14, it says, '

Therefore the Lord himself will give you a sign: The virgin will conceive and give birth to a son, and will call him Immanuel.'

And then in the New Testament, in Matthew chapter 1:20, it tells about when Joseph was hesitant to take Mary as his wife."

But after he had considered this, an angel of the Lord appeared to him in a dream and said, "Joseph, son of David, do not be afraid to take Mary home as your wife, because what is conceived in her is from the Holy Spirit. She will give birth to a son, and you are to give him the name Jesus, because he will save his people from their sins. All this took place to fulfill what the Lord had said through the prophet: 'The virgin will conceive and give birth to a son, and they will call him Immanuel' (which means "God with us").

"There was another in chapter 2 of Matthew.

After Jesus was born in Bethlehem in Judea, during the time of King Herod, Magi from the east came to Jerusalem and asked, 'Where is the one who has been born king of the Jews? We saw his star when it rose and have come to worship him.'"

"When King Herod heard this he was disturbed, and all Jerusalem with him. When he had called together all the people's chief priests and teachers of the law, he asked them where the Messiah was to be born. 'In Bethlehem in Judea,' they replied, 'for this is what the prophet has written: But you, Bethlehem, in the land of Judah, are by no means least among the rulers of Judah; for out of you will come a ruler who will shepherd my people Israel.'

That was prophesied in Micah 5:2."

"My point here is this. The Old Testament of the Bible prophesied these things long before they came to be. The Magi were expecting the Messiah, which is Jesus. They got on their camels, brought gifts for him, and traveled a long way to see him. But most people weren't paying attention. Likewise, the disappearances were prophesied, and we weren't paying attention."

"The first scripture we are going to read about the disappearances is 1 Corinthians 15:51. 'Listen, I tell you a mystery. We will not all sleep, but we will all be changed- in a flash, in the twinkling of an eye, at the last trumpet. For the trumpet will sound...'"

"Now let's stop there! Did any of you hear a loud sound, like thunder, or a trumpet, on Thanksgiving Day when the people disappeared?" About half of the people in the room raised their hands. "Yes, I heard it too! It was the trumpet that was prophesied or the voice of the archangel."

"'For the trumpet will sound, the dead will be raised imperishable, and we will be changed. For the perishable (that's us, we can perish) must cloth itself with the imperishable, and the mortal with immortality.'"

"So what we are learning here is that when we heard that loud sound, dead people who were believers, who had put their hope in Jesus to take away their sins, suddenly were taken up to heaven and were given their immortal, eternal bodies. My Grandma and Grandpa Ashcraft, are not in their graves any longer."

"I'll tell you another thing that I learned," said Jackson. "My grandma and grandpa were not sleeping in the ground all these years! Their spirits, their minds, were awake and aware, in heaven with God and Jesus, since the day they died."

"Now my brother Harold's in-laws, their whole family of believers, didn't die at all. We were there. They just disappeared, suddenly. They were changed on the way up and met Jesus in the air, when we heard that loud sound. Can you imagine how wonderful that would be, to not die at all, but just go to heaven?"

"Here is another scripture about this Rapture that took place. 1 Thessalonians 4:13."

Brothers and sisters, we do not want you to be uninformed about those who sleep in death, so that you do not grieve like the rest of mankind, who have no hope. For we believe that Jesus died and rose again, and so we believe that God will bring with Jesus those who have fallen asleep in him. According to the Lord's word, we tell you that we who are still alive, who are left until the coming of the Lord, will certainly not precede those who have fallen asleep. For the Lord himself will come down from heaven, with a loud command, with the voice of the archangel and with the

trumpet call of God, and the dead in Christ will rise first.
After that, we who are still alive and who are left will be
caught up together with them in the clouds to meet the Lord
in the air. And so we will be with the Lord forever. Therefore,
encourage one another with these words.

"Now this was very good news for them!" said Jackson. "But we did not make it! This is not good news at all for us! We could sit here and cry for hours that we missed out. But that's not going to help at all. But all is not lost. We still have a chance to be with God and Jesus forever."

"Are we paying attention now?" asked Jackson. "Are we going to be prepared for what is to come? We can do the most important thing of all. We can put our hope in Jesus, who is God's own Son. Right after Jesus was killed, and after he arose, and after he went up to heaven, in the resurrection, his disciples told us what to do. Listen to this when Peter and the other disciples were asked, in Acts 2:37, 'Brothers, what shall we do?'"

"This is what Peter answered in Acts 2:38, 'Repent and be baptized, every one of you, in the name of Jesus Christ for the forgiveness of your sins. And you will receive the gift of the Holy Spirit. The promise is for you and your children, and for all who are far off- for all whom the Lord our God will call.'"

"So right now, my brother Royal and I are going to do this most important thing in our lives. I'm going to baptize Royal and he's going to baptize me." So the two of them met at the baptistry, while everyone else watched. They took off their shoes and their belts, and emptied their pockets. Alan came out to meet them with towels. So Jackson and Royal went down into the water.

Jackson asked, "Royal do you believe that Jesus is the Christ, the son of the living God, and that he died for our sins?"

"Yes," answered Royal. "And I want to be baptized, in Jesus' name, for the forgiveness of my sins and the gift of the Holy Spirit."

So Jackson lowered Royal into the water and helped him back up. Then they traded places and Royal baptized Jackson.

"Now any and all of you who want to confess your faith in Jesus, can be baptized as well," said Jackson. "We did this with our clothes on, but some of you might want to wear a robe, to keep your clothes dry."

"That's right," said Alan. "We have a men's and a women's changing room and robes back here for those of you who want to prepare, and plenty of towels for everyone. My wife will direct you to the dressing rooms. If you want to get baptized as you are, step right up! And if you don't mind, I'm going first!"

Alan pulled off his shoes and tie and belt and laid his phone, keys, and wallet with them, and stepped forward and was baptized. His friend Max went next. After that most of the people, along with their kids, got baptized. Jackson got to baptize his father and his brother Harold, and Royal got to baptize his mother. Alan's wife went last.

Alan had prepared a communion mediation, so they all took communion together.

Jackson announced, "I'm not going to lie to you folks. We have terrible times coming, and we may all die, but if we do die, those of us who put our faith in Jesus today are going to heaven. This Wednesday night, at 7 pm, in that big room over there, we will sit around tables, and together we will learn what we need to do in the next seven years, which is called the Tribulation. Now the Tribulation could begin before then, or it could be years away. Bring your Bibles."

Then Royal said a closing prayer, thanking God, in Jesus' name that their future was now safe for eternity, whether they lived or died.

Alan held out a plate and announced, "If you want to get this church going again, you can make an offering." Most of the people put some money into the plate.

Later in the afternoon, Harold and Cynthia went over to visit the family. Cynthia was feeling better, and she understood that she missed quite a morning. Jackson was at his corner, preparing to teach the people and prepare them for what comes next. Royal felt like he needed to learn more about Jesus, from beginning to the present time. He was working in another area of the room. John was reading through the book of Genesis, and planned to work his way through the whole Bible.

Helen shared with the family that she had just had a discussion with Megan, Jenna's neighbor and best friend in New Jersey.

"What?" asked Cynthia. "How could you possibly know Jenna's best friend in New Jersey?"

"We went over to Cheryl's house after the disappearances to find some books about the Bible. While we were there, we walked around the house, to make sure they didn't have any pets. Upstairs, in the girl's room, I found a cell phone. So I took it with me. It turned out that it was Jenna's, and the only number in the phone was her best friend Megan's. So I called her and talked to her and told her about Jenna disappearing."

"You would think I would know about it if Jenna had a best friend. That must be the same girl who showed up with her mother and told us that Jenna ran away to Ohio," said Cynthia.

"Well just as I thought, she was really worried when Jenna didn't call her after the disappearances," said Helen. "I was able to tell her for sure that she disappeared. So this time I called her to see how she was doing. And you know what, Jackson? Megan, Jenna's best friend in New Jersey, said they really need some help learning about the tribulation. She said she can't sleep at night because she's scared about what's coming."

"I'm scared too!" said Royal. "We should all be scared!"

"I'll call her and talk to her dad," said Jackson. "If they can find an empty church building, or even a church that lost its leaders, I could teach them the same thing I just taught. And I could stay for a few days, and do the Bible study. Hey, I could stay at your house, couldn't I Harold? It's right next door."

"I guess so," said Harold. "Um, I didn't tell Cynthia what we all did this morning."

They all looked up from their studies, wondering why Harold didn't tell Cynthia. "Is it because we didn't include Cynthia, or is it because you didn't want her to know that you did it Harold?" asked Jackson.

"What did you all do?" asked Cynthia.

"We all became Christians and we got baptized," said Harold. "And we're hoping you will do that too."

"I can't. I just can't! I don't deserve forgiveness. I was a terrible mother! I was mean and unloving and selfish! And I was a terrible daughter too! My parents never did anything but good and I repaid them by rejecting their discipline and moving away. I never even sent my mom a Mothers' Day card or a birthday card. We never went home for Thanksgiving or Christmas. Instead, we spent our time getting drunk and hanging out with people who didn't even like us. I wasted my whole life. Why would Jesus save me?" Cynthia covered her face and sat down.

Harold ran over and sat down next to Cynthia and put his arm around her. "You weren't that bad Cynthia Dear," he said. "And you were always so good to me."

Jackson said, "We are all sinners. Jesus died and took on all of our sins. He was whipped and he had a crown of thorns jammed down on his head. And he hung on the cross. He could have stopped it all, but he hung there and died, because he loves us. And there isn't anything we did that his blood won't cover. Cynthia, it sounds like you are already sorry for your sins!"

"I am," said Cynthia. "And I can't even tell Jenna how sorry I am. And I can't ever tell Mom and Dad that I am sorry. And you guys, John and Helen. I'm so sorry that you didn't get to enjoy Jenna."

"Are you ready to put your faith in Jesus for the forgiveness of your sins, and the gift of the Holy Spirit and the promise of eternal life with God?" asked Jackson.

"Yes, I want that. Are you sure he will forgive me? Even me?" asked Cynthia.

"Maybe we can go to that church and baptize Cynthia," said Jackson.

"Why don't we do that here?" said John. "Let's go out to the hot tub? Do you want to get baptized Cynthia?"

"Can we do that? I mean it is wintertime," said Cynthia.

"The hot tub is all clean and warm," said Helen. "We use it a lot. I'll grab some towels."

"Would you take me home to change clothes afterward, Harold?" Cynthia asked.

"Of course I will!" said Harold.

So the whole family went outside with a 32 degree temperature to baptize Cynthia. Harold got in the water with Cynthia and helped

Jackson lower her into the water and lift her back up. Helen cried and said, "This is the best day ever! I wish your mom could see this John!"

"Yes. My mom's dying wish and prayer came true. Everyone in her family is a Christian now!" said John.

So Harold and Cynthia, wrapped up in towels, went out to their car, and drove to their new home, given to them in faith, by Fred and Evelyn Jones.

———

Harold and Cynthia parked in their new driveway and walked to their backdoor.

Angie was taking out the trash from Cheryl's house, and she said, "What on earth happened to you two?"

"I have to get in a hot shower," said Cynthia. "Can you talk to her?"

"Yes, of course Dearest," said Harold. Then he turned to Angie and asked, "What can I do for you?"

"Oh, I just wondered why you guys were so wet," said Angie. "Did you get in an accident of some kind?"

"No," said Harold. "We were baptized. I did it this morning at a church, and Cynthia was baptized a little later in my parents' hot tub."

"That's nice," said Angie. "But I was just wondering if you and Cynthia decided if we can have this house."

"Well, you can't have the house. It was given to my wife to use as she sees fit. But we are going to let you stay here with a couple requirements. First of all, you are to take very good care of the place, inside and out. It has to be neat and clean and not cluttered. Next, you are to pay the utilities on the house and never be late. Third, you are to maintain the outside property of this house and the one next door that we are living in. That's it, there is no rent. So you will have to mow the yard in the summer and weed the flower beds. You will have to rake leaves in the fall and shovel the driveway in the winter."

"There is one more thing," said Harold, "but it is not required, just recommended. My brothers are conducting a Bible study this Wednesday at 7 pm. Cynthia and I will be attending. We are hoping to learn how to live and survive the next several years as Christians. Are you interested?"

"I'm not Christian, I'm Jewish, and Ernie isn't religious at all. We weren't planning on paying utilities to live here and we certainly weren't expecting to work that much," said Angie.

"Who did you think was going to pay your electric bill and your heating bill? And water, sewer, and trash pickup aren't free. We can cancel the internet and cable TV if you don't want to pay for those things," said Harold.

"Hold on. I'll have to discuss all of this with Ernie, but I can tell you, we won't be attending that Bible study," said Angie. "We won't have time with all of that work we have to do."

"Didn't you say that you're a school bus driver?" asked Harold. "Surely you make enough to pay utilities."

"I was going to quit," said Angie.

"Who was going to buy your food and other needs?" asked Harold.

"My mother and Ernie's mother live with us and pay for our food," said Angie. "They both get a pension."

"Well, don't you have a house to sell, that you were living in?" asked Harold.

"We were renting that place," said Angie. "I'm kind of disappointed. We thought we were going to live the easy life from now on."

"There isn't going to be an easy life for any of us from now on," said Harold. "Didn't you ever hear of the tribulation? My brothers just told me a little, but it's going to be horrifying. You need to come Wednesday night just to hear about it.'

"Oh come on. I don't believe that conspiracy stuff," said Angie.

"Well, you believe that people disappeared, don't you?" asked Harold.

"They could have all been kidnapped or something," said Angie. "No one knows where they went, according to the news."

"Why don't you come Wednesday night and find out what is going on in the world?" suggested Harold.

"No thanks," said Angie. "I have to figure out who is going to pay those bills." And she turned around and went in the house.

Chapter 19

Jackson had promised his mother that he would call Megan's father on Jenna's phone.

"Hello Mrs. Ashcraft," answered Megan.

"This is her son, Jackson, and I was Jenna's uncle." said Jackson. "I promised my mother that I would call and talk to your father. She said that your family wanted to know more about the tribulation."

"Just a minute," said Megan. "I'll get him."

"This is Jimmy. Megan says you are a relative of Jenna's."

"That's right," said Jackson. "My brother, Harold, owns the house next door to you. He's currently visiting us in Ohio."

"What can I do for you?" asked Jimmy.

"Well your daughter told my mom that you folks are having trouble understanding the tribulation, and your daughter is having trouble sleeping," said Jackson. "I'm preparing a Bible study for this Wednesday night at 6 pm and it's all about the tribulation. I can come some other time and teach you and maybe others what we are learning about the tribulation. And I can stay next door at Harold and Cynthia's house."

"Where do you live in Ohio, Jackson?" asked Jimmy.

"We live in Canton, Ohio," said Jackson.

"I have an aunt that I haven't seen in several years who lives in Canal Fulton, Ohio," said Jimmy. "We can go visit her and go to your Bible study on Wednesday. Can we bring our girls?"

"You are welcome to bring your children if you want," said Jackson. "But the tribulation is going to be terrible. This study could really scare your children."

"Well, I might leave my younger one with my aunt, but Megan is seventeen, and she wants to learn all she can about Jesus and God and the next seven years," said Jimmy.

Jackson gave Jimmy the address of the church and his phone number, and Jimmy gave Jackson his own phone number.

———

Jackson and Royal worked many hours to prepare for the Wednesday evening Bible study. Jackson prepared every point he planned to make from the scripture, and Royal prepared a worksheet for everyone to fill in, with scripture references included, for the people to look up later, as they need them. Jackson was sure they will need them. But then Jackson thought of his grandmother Ashcraft in heaven, and came up with another plan.

When Wednesday arrived, the entire Ashcraft family was at the church two hours early, arranging tables in the fellowship hall, squeezing seven chairs around each table made for six, and putting three Bibles at each table, in case some people don't have one. Royal and Helen put the worksheets at each place, and soon they were prepared to teach about the tribulation to a crowd of 154 people.

The first to arrive were Jimmy, Kara, and Megan and Mindy from New Jersey, and Jimmy's aunt and uncle, who also wanted to learn about the next seven years. Helen gave Megan a big hug and told her how thankful she was that she had been there for Jenna all those years. Megan was frightened when she was introduced to Harold and Cynthia. But Harold assured her that they are Christians now and they are embarrassed about what they were like in the past.

Then the people started filing into the room. Every table was soon full and people were lining up around the room. Cynthia jumped up and began giving a worksheet to people standing.

Jackson had given each of his family members a job in the presentation. Jackson began with a prayer, that God would give them all wisdom tonight and in the coming years. Then Jackson gave a nod to his father, who stood right up.

"Hello, I am John Ashcraft, Jackson's father. First I want to talk to you about The Replacement Theology that many of our students were indoctrinated with in college by ultra-liberal professors. The Replacement Theology teaches that the Jews, also called the Israelites, were replaced as God's chosen people by the Christians. Now don't get me wrong, God loves us Christians. We are cherished and cared for. Now get ready to follow along on your worksheet. This is what the Apostle Paul said about this in the book of Romans, chapter 11, verse 25.

'I do not want you to be ignorant of this mystery, brothers and sisters, so that you may not be conceited: Israel has experienced a hardening in part until the full number of the Gentiles has come in, and in this way all Israel will be saved.'"

"So we feel certain that we are among the final groups of Gentiles, which means anyone who is not a Jew, to come in, and become Christians. It's too bad we weren't paying attention earlier," said John Ashcraft, "and then we would not be facing the 'wrath to come.' Follow along now on your worksheet. 1 Thessalonians 1:10. 'And to wait for his Son from heaven, whom he raised from the dead- Jesus, who rescues us from the coming wrath.' So we missed out on the rescue, the rapture, also called the disappearances, and now we are coming into a time of wrath."

Royal was the next person to come forward to speak. "My name is Royal Ashcraft and I'm Jackson and Harold's brother, and John and Helen's son. We don't know when the tribulation will begin, but it might be soon. It also could be several years before it begins. The tribulation, although scary for us, is an important time for the Jews. God will protect them, and through God's miraculous provision and protection, they will believe."

"A time is coming when the people of Israel will need God's protection," continued Royal. "According to Ezekiel 38 and 39, there will be an invasion of Israel by many countries. Maybe you have noticed an increase in anti-Semitism in our country. You hear it occasionally from our liberal members of congress. This invasion, according to the book of Ezekiel will come from Russia, the leader, Iran, Libya, Syria, and Turkey. Also possible countries included in the invasion are Kazakhstan, Kyrgyzstan, Uzbekistan, Turkmenistan, Tajikistan, Afghanistan, Iraq, Sudan, Algeria and Tunisia, and maybe others. What do most of these countries have in common besides the hatred of Israel? The answer is that they are Muslim," said Royal.

"That's right," said Jackson. "Remember last June, July, and August when many angry men and women joined in the riots, looting and plundering and carrying off whatever they could find? This will be similar, but many times bigger, as countries join in and cover the land like a cloud. Do you think that all of the women and children and old people of that Russian coalition will be safe at home, watching on their TV's and phones and urging them on? No! Ezekiel 39:6 says, 'I will send fire on Magog and on those who live in safety in the coastlands, and they will know that I am the Lord.' So as you can see from the scripture, if we understand it right, God will send fire and calamity on the families back home of those who go to attack Israel."

"Follow along with me now in the book of Ezekiel 38:14," said Royal.

This is what the Sovereign Lord says: In that day, when my people Israel are living in safety, will you not take notice of it? You will come from your place in the far north, you and many nations with you, all of them riding on horses, a great horde, a mighty army. You will advance against my land, so that the nations may know me when I am proved holy through you before their eyes…. This is what will happen in that day: When Gog attacks the land of Israel, my hot anger will be aroused, declares the Sovereign Lord. In my zeal and fiery wrath I declare that at that time there shall be a great earthquake in the land of Israel. The fish in the sea, the birds in the sky, the beasts of the field, every creature that moves along the ground, and all the people on the face of the earth will tremble at my presence. The mountains will be overturned, the cliffs will crumble and every wall will fall to the ground. I will summon a sword against Gog on all my

mountains, declares the Sovereign Lord. Every man's sword
will be against his brother.

And then Royal said, "Remember, these invaders will be speaking many different languages, so when God makes every man's sword be against his brother, they won't even be able to argue about it."

Jackson said, "Let's continue where Royal just left off, on 38:22. 'I will execute judgment on him with plague and bloodshed; I will pour down torrents of rain, hailstones and burning sulfur on him and on his troops and on the many nations with him. And so I will show my greatness and my holiness, and I will make myself known in the sight of many nations. Then they will know that I am the Lord.'"

Then Royal continued in Ezekiel 39:4.

"On the mountains of Israel you will fall, you and all your troops and the nations with you. I will give you as food to all kinds of carrion birds and to the wild animals...vs. 12. For seven months the Israelites will be burying them in order to cleanse the land. Vs. 9 Then those who live in the towns of Israel will go out and use the weapons for fuel and burn them up- the small and large shields, the bows and arrows, the war clubs and spears. For seven years, they will use them for fuel."

"I gave this scripture to Royal, because he has been freaking out thinking that we Christians would be running from wild animals, and it could just be the enemies of God, who will suffer from that," said Jackson.

"Thank you Jackson," said Royal. "Now maybe I can sleep a little better."

"What we don't know yet is when this invasion will take place," said Jackson. "We think it could be soon, and maybe the tribulation won't start until the people of Israel have finished burying the dead bodies and finished the first three and a half years of burning weapons. If that is true, we might have four years until the tribulation begins and that gives us more time to win other people to Christ and save them from eternal suffering."

"Our brother Harold is going to tell you why we think the tribulation will happen after the great Ezekiel invasion of Israel," said Royal.

"We think that after all of the Muslim nations have been destroyed, the Israelites will be free to build their temple, since the site of the new temple is occupied by the Muslim Dome of the Rock," said Harold. "A man will rise to be a world leader, and he will be the antichrist. He might offer to make an agreement with Israel for peace and protection, and they might be eager to sign on if he offers to move the Dome of the Rock. Let's look at Daniel 9:27, 'He will confirm a covenant with many for one *seven.*' That means it's a contract for seven years. When they sign that agreement, that will be the beginning of the tribulation period, and that is when our trouble will begin."

A woman from one of the tables went up to Helen. She was very shook up and showed her a text on her phone. Helen ran up to Jackson and showed him the message. Harold had stopped talking when he saw his mother looking upset. Jackson looked at his friend from the church and asked, "Alan do we have a working TV with cable around here?"

Alan pointed to the side of the room and said, "I'll get the remote." There before their eyes was a scene from a country across the world, Iran. Men were dressed in military clothing, others were dressed in jeans and T-shirts or hoodies. They were shouting excitedly and carrying clubs and baseball bats and some had signs. Then the news switched to Turkey where the scene looked very similar. In Moscow, there were tanks on the road and many people were cheering, like it was a parade.

Then the station showed a scene in Minnesota, where rioters were filling the streets with signs that said "Death to Israel" and "Push them into the Sea!" The newscaster then said, "Now look at these scenes from airports around the country, as young people, male and female, are buying tickets to go to various cities in the Middle East: Tehran, Istanbul, Baghdad, Alexandria, Kabul, Cairo and Damascus, to name a few."

Then they featured a congresswoman from Michigan saying, "If you are traveling to Israel, remember, don't trample the gardens, don't burn the houses, and don't hurt the land, only kill the people."

"As you can see, the Ezekiel 38 and 39 invasion of Israel has started, and many even from the US are hoping to go there and participate. They haven't studied what God has in store for them as they travel to Israel," said Jackson. "Can any of you name one thing God will do to them as they march or ride to Israel?"

Two children raised their hands. One said that there will be a terrible earthquake. The other one said the cliffs will crumble and walls will fall.

Many other people raised their hands. Jackson pointed to each and they would answer: earthquake, plagues, hail, burning sulfur and they will kill each other with their swords.

"And Royal, what two do you remember the most?" asked Jackson.

"I wouldn't go anywhere near the Middle East right now," said Royal, "because God is going to invite the birds of prey and wild animals to come and feast on their dead bodies."

Then the news went back to the scene in Russia. The tanks were turning around and a news caster said that Russia wants the wealth in Israel and the technological secrets, so they just agreed to go in on horseback and aircraft and save the land and property for the Palestinians.

A man raised his hand and asked, "What do the Iranians, Turks, and all the other countries over there want?"

"They want revenge," said Jackson. "They hate the people of Israel. I'm going to end our study here, but we will meet here Sunday morning at 10 am and again next Wednesday evening at 6 pm. Don't forget to watch the news this week. Prophecy is unfolding right in front of our eyes."

After the Bible study, the Ashcraft family stayed around and talked with the people who attended. The family from New Jersey came up to Jackson and Royal.

"We are going to stick around for a week," said Jimmy, Megan's father. "I have two weeks of vacation, and I can't think of a better use of our time than learning what's going on in the world and being prepared."

"Have you accepted the Lord as your savior," asked Royal.

Jackson slapped himself on the forehead and exclaimed, "I forgot to offer an invitation!"

"It's not too late," said Jimmy. "Most of the people are still here."

"Excuse me everyone," announced Jackson. "Are any of you ready to confess the Lord as your personal savior, and get baptized?"

Although many people had been baptized on Sunday, there were plenty more who wanted to go forward. So they all went to the baptistry, and welcomed even more people into God's kingdom, including Jenna's friend Megan from New Jersey and her family.

Chapter 20

Back at John and Helen Ashcraft's home, the family sat around the living room, watching the news. A big map of the Middle East was on the screen, and it featured many countries preparing to invade Israel, from northern Africa to western Asia, and southern Europe. They were coming from all directions. There was a general agreement among the invaders to protect the land of Israel and the technology, but to kill the people. For that reason, many soldiers were coming with old-fashioned swords and shields. Many people had bows and arrows. Some were coming on horses, but many were coming on foot! And they were plundering, rioting, and stealing on their way to Israel.

Helen and Cynthia were sitting off to the side of the room, away from the TV.

"Helen," said Cynthia, "I really do regret so much about our lives. I hate our relationship with Jenna. I hate that I wasn't friends with my own sister Cheryl. I regret that I wasn't close to my parents and to you and John. I know God will forgive me. Jackson said that God will remove our sins as far as the east is from the west. That's in Psalm 103. And I am so grateful for that. But will you forgive me Helen? Do you think my mom and dad will ever forgive us? Can you forgive us for keeping Jenna away from you?"

"I can," said Helen. "But I want you to know that I was so jealous of my friends who have grandchildren. And then I only got two visits with Jenna."

"I'm so sorry," said Cynthia, "but I have to tell you that I'm thankful that she's safe and sound where she is, and according to Jackson, we might get to see her in a few years."

Harold came over and told Cynthia that he was tired and wanted to go to their new home, so they took off.

Once at home, Harold and Cynthia pulled into the driveway and there was a huge storage pod in Angie and Ernie's driveway next door. They decided to knock on the door and find out what was going on.

"Why is there storage pod in the driveway?" asked Harold.

Angie was crying and couldn't really talk. Ernie came to the door and said, "Mom, come meet Harold and Cynthia, the folks who are letting us stay in this house for now. This is Angie's mother."

"Nice to meet you," she said. "My name is Esther. We are having a family emergency, but we don't want to trouble you nice people."

"Oh no," said Harold. "Is someone moving out?"

"No one is moving out, but more people are moving in," said Ernie. "The good news is, they can probably help pay for the utilities."

"How many more people are moving in," asked Cynthia. "There are already ten of you, right?"

"Yes, there are ten of us, and there could be eight more, but we certainly didn't plan this," said Angie. "My brothers' family was planning to move to Israel. They had sold their house and purchased airline tickets, and then they heard on the news that Israel is going to be attacked by many countries. People all over the world, even America, hate us. And now they are heading there to kill everyone in Israel and take over the land."

"Not everybody hates Jews Angie," said her mom. "Right now, my son and family just don't know whether they will need their stuff soon or not for a long time. My dear husband and I always dreamed of moving to Israel, and then he passed last year. I was going to join my son's family once they got settled, and now I guess the whole move is canceled, and there might not be an Israel to immigrate to."

Harold and Cynthia looked at each other, and didn't know where to begin. Harold quickly texted Jackson and told him to get Royal and maybe Dad and get over to Harold and Cynthia's, to advise a family about moving to Israel tomorrow.

"Have your son and his family come in here and talk to us," said Harold.

Ernie ran upstairs and came back with two adults and six children from teens to toddlers and introduced them to Harold and Cynthia.

"So are you people Jewish?" asked Harold.

"Yes we are," said Angie's brother. "We have been planning this trip for the last five years. We had a whole planeload from our area near Cleveland. Some say they will not ever go now, and others say maybe later if there are any people alive, and our good friends are still going."

"Please sit down," said Harold. "I sent a quick text to my family. Cynthia, should we wait until they get here or go ahead and start?"

"What's to talk about?" asked Angie. "They will be killed immediately if they go there."

"Angie, please," said her sister-in-law. "You'll scare the children."

"If you go to Israel, you will not be killed," said Harold. "God is going to protect the people of Israel."

"And not only that," said Cynthia. "God is going to kill off all of the attackers."

"How can you even suggest those things? We even heard there are some people going there from Cleveland," said Angie. "And they are going there to kill Jews!"

"Why don't we read the scripture while we wait for our family," said Harold. "Do you guys all have a Bible?"

"I saw two of them up in the girl's room," said one of their kids.

John and Helen Ashcraft arrived and Helen knew there were Bibles upstairs.

"We came here after the disappearances and I saw many Bibles around the house," said Helen. "Why don't you all go find a Bible? You'll be glad you did."

In a few minutes, all but the youngest child in the family was sitting around the big room with a Bible. "OK," said Harold. "Everyone turn to the book of Ezekiel, chapter 38. It's past the middle of the Bible."

Helen and Harold went around helping everyone and just as they were ready to begin reading the two chapters, Jackson and Royal arrived.

"I hear that some of you are planning to immigrate to Israel," said Jackson. "What an exciting time to go there."

"I'm glad you think so," said Joshua, Angie's brother. "Would you like to go in our place?"

"If I was one of the Children of Israel, I would be on the first plane going there," said Jackson. "I have to tell you, that I think you will be safer in Israel, even with the coming invasion, than you will be here in the United States."

"Well I find that hard to believe," said Angie.

Jackson read Ezekiel 38: 9 about the coalition,

"You and all your troops and the many nations with you will go up, advancing like a storm; you will be like a cloud covering the land."

In the room where they sat, the television was on with the sound down. They all looked up and saw a satellite view of the land of Israel and the nations surrounding it, and what they saw was like a cloud, going from many nations zeroing in on Israel. Many of the family gasped.

Then the family read through the two chapters, covering the way God will wipe out the invaders, with an earthquake, causing cliffs to crumble and walls to fall. They read about a time when the invaders' swords will be against other fellow invaders, and when God will cause plagues and bloodshed, torrents of rain, hailstones, and burning sulfur, on the invading countries and on the many nations with them. They made sure the Jewish family knew about the birds of prey and wild beasts feasting on the attacking enemy and that God will send fire, not only on the invaders, but also on their families watching from their homes.

Royal asked, "When were you all supposed to fly to Israel? Did you cancel your tickets?"

"No, I didn't cancel our tickets," said Joshua. "I just couldn't with so many of our friends going."

"So are we going or not, Daddy," asked one of his children.

"It sure sounds like God is going to protect us because we are his chosen people," said Joshua.

"I do have one warning for you," said Jackson. "Don't wait too long to accept that Jesus is the Messiah, the son of God."

"We are Jews, not Christians," said Joshua's mother.

The whole family looked at Jackson to see what he would say. "Not only will the Jews finally accept that Jesus is the Christ, the son of God, but 144,000 of you will become evangelists, spreading the good news about Jesus, and winning Jews and Gentiles to the Kingdom of God," said Jackson. "You might be one of those chosen, and your two sons might also be chosen."

"Will God still protect us from the invaders if we become Christians?" asked Joshua.

"Of course. It's just a matter of time until you all will believe," said Jackson.

The family sat there, silently thinking about what Jackson said.

Royal said, "You should have been there, in the house next door, when fifteen people disappeared right in front of our eyes. We were so shook up that we moved back home with Mom and Dad. Think about this. If it was prophesied in the Bible that people would actually disappear when Jesus came and took them to heaven, then this invasion that we see happening, will be just as the Bible says, and you people will be protected if you go to Israel."

"So I guess we have a choice. Jump on that plane tomorrow and go to Israel, or stay here and become Christians, right?" asked Joshua's son Saul.

"No," said Jackson. "You can do both."

"Dad, I saw someone disappear and I kept quiet about it," said Mark, another son. "I was terrified and I didn't say a word."

"Well now we know that those who disappeared are safe in heaven. Let's go to Israel and become Christians with the others there," said Joshua.

"Wonderful," said Royal. "You know, it will take seven months to bury the bodies of the invaders, what's left of them.

"We have to make sure we all get to the airport in the morning by 8:00 am," said Joshua.

"Are you saying we're going for sure?" asked Joshua's wife Eva.

"Yes!" said Joshua. "We're going to Israel."

One of Joshua's girls asked him, "Daddy, will we still be Jews if we become Christians?"

Joshua looked over at Jackson, and Jackson said, "You will be Messianic Jews, which means that you believe that Jesus is the Messiah, God's own son. What could be better than that?"

"Can we keep in touch with your family?" asked Joshua. They exchanged phone numbers and Joshua promised to contact them after they land and know the status of things.

Chapter 21

The Ashcraft brothers planned to stay up all night, watching the cloud of invaders approach Israel, not because they were worried, but because they wanted to see God's Word in action. On the station they were watching, a reporter approached a bunch of Americans, passing through Jordan. The invaders were young, mostly male, and carrying clubs and ball bats. They were showing off for the camera, hitting their clubs, and shouting that they were here to kill some Jews. The reporter asked about some others that were going off on a different path. They said their friends were doing a little looting on the way, after all, they need food and drink!

Then the station switched to Egypt. Many soldiers were marching to Israel and were carrying bows and arrows. The people standing along the roadway were shouting to the soldiers and asking, "Have you come to plunder? Are you going to carry off silver and gold?" But the soldiers were not amused. In fact they weren't feeling good at all.

The reporter asked, "Are you soldiers ok?" Just then the soldiers stopped marching and began throwing up. "Yuck," said the reporter. He looked at his cameraman and said, "Let's get out of here before we catch whatever they're carrying." As they looked back, the soldiers were falling to the ground and losing consciousness, right in the middle of the road.

"You know, Jackson," said Royal. "This is just like reading Ezekiel. I think I'll go to bed and start watching again in the morning. We know exactly how this is going to go."

"I guess you're right," said Jackson. "I can barely keep my eyes open. This way, the time will go faster until Joshua calls to tell us what is going on there in Israel."

Joshua's mom, Esther, called Helen the next morning and told her that their family arranged for the storage pod to be picked up and stored at a place nearby. She also said that the kids had packed their bags and showered the night before, and they told her that they slept all night without any worry. Esther said that Joshua called from the airport to say good-bye, and that most of their friends and neighbors showed up for the move to Israel. Esther said that she still plans to follow them in a few months when they get settled in a house. Helen shared this good news with Jackson and Royal the next morning when they were up and about.

"Well it is 10:00 am, so Joshua's family is probably taking off right now," said Jackson. "I wonder what has happened through the night on the other side of the world." They turned on the TV and were surprised that the station they watched at bedtime was still focused on the happenings in Egypt. A different reporter was on duty, with a different cameraman.

"This is Amir Jacobson on the East -West Highway in Egypt, picking up where last night's crew left off. The group of soldiers on this road last night were hit with some kind of plague and now they are all dead. The Egyptians report that they did call an emergency squad, but the soldiers were all dead before the ambulance arrived. The rescue workers were ordered not to touch or move the bodies. About an hour later, a huge truck arrived and three workers, dressed in hazmat suits, threw the bodies into a truck, and drove away with them. It was determined that the soldiers were from Libya and were headed for Israel. And now our station will feature a group from Iran."

Royal turned down the TV, and asked Jackson if it's right for them to be celebrating the deaths of so many Muslims.

"I was wondering the same thing," said Jackson. "Last night Joshua shared something with me. He said that many Muslims live in Israel peacefully, but most just want the Israelites dead and gone. The hatred goes back thousands of years. Joshua thinks that they know they are fighting against God, but they do it anyway. The best thing we can do is save as many people as possible. Who knows, we might rescue some Muslims if we persevere. I think it is appropriate for us to mourn those who die, but we know that God's judgement is perfect."

The brothers watched the same station for hours as they interviewed many traveling to Israel. As the station went to countries farther north, they saw many on horseback with sophisticated weapons. Suddenly Jackson's cell phone rang.

"Royal, this could be the call we've been waiting for," said Jackson.

"Sorry I didn't call sooner," said Joshua. "We just experienced the biggest, strongest earthquake. We have been dizzy ever since we were bounced up and down and side to side. I have to tell my mother that the airport here will be closed for a long time, because the runways have been damaged beyond repair and the airport itself is demolished. We managed to get outside just as it was starting."

"We will certainly check in on your mom from time to time," said Jackson.

"Please check on my sister Angie too," said Joshua. "She's always been difficult to reach about God. And please try to save my baby sister Janene, too. She's made some mistakes, but she's a good mother. She doesn't get any help from the kids' dad."

"I'll try," said Jackson. "Angie's husband Ernie seems to have some sense about him."

"Yes," said Joshua. "He's a good guy!"

"Was the country of Israel damaged much in the earthquake?" asked Jackson.

"I'm sure there was a lot of damage," said Joshua.

"What is the mood of the people in Israel with invaders coming to kill them from every direction?" asked Jackson.

"Most of the people here are prepared to defend our country, with every kind of weapon when needed," said Joshua, "but so far they haven't needed to do anything."

"Well, you know that's because God is taking care of it. Where are you going to stay tonight?" asked Jackson.

"There are apartments for our family and all of our friends," said Joshua. "I hope they haven't been damaged. We will travel around Israel and decide where we want to settle. You know, my family looks really worried. The sky is getting very dark. I think we're in for a storm."

"Get under cover, fast! The storms that are coming will be very dangerous," said Jackson. "Watch out for hail and torrents of rain."

"Oh that's right," said Joshua. "You know the future."

"Did you take those Bibles with you?" asked Jackson.

"Yes, we all took one," said Joshua.

"Well then read Ezekiel 38 and 39," said Jackson. "Then you'll know the future."

"I have say good-bye for now," said Joshua. "Here comes the storm!"

———

Jackson and Royal looked at each other. Royal said, "It's really happening, isn't it? Everything is just the way the Bible describes it."

"Yes," said Jackson. "The Bible doesn't say that every person living in Israel will be safe, so I'm sure going to be praying for them."

"Oh I think they will all be safe," said Royal. "But the ones in the coalition coming against them are going to be obliterated. Imagine the invading soldiers going across a field, and then being chased and eaten by wild animals. I don't want to watch that on some ambitious reporter's watch. The reporter and the cameraman could get gobbled up too!"

"I know this should ruin my appetite, but we haven't had anything to eat for hours," said Jackson. "Where are Mom and Dad?"

The boys went to the kitchen and began snacking on whatever they could find, cereal, chips, and yogurt. Finally they heard the garage door, and in walked John and Helen with their arms full of groceries.

"Hurray, groceries," said Royal. "We're starving!"

"Not so fast," said Helen. "We're having guests for dinner tonight."

"Who's coming and what are we serving?" asked Jackson.

"Well Harold and Cynthia, of course, but also our New Jersey friends, Jimmy, Kara, Megan, and Manda," said Helen. "They are going home Thursday after they attend our Wednesday night Bible study. They will be here at 6:00, so we need you two to pitch in and help."

The guests arrived and they had a nice dinner, with Helen getting to know Megan and Manda. Megan forgot that Harold and Cynthia were sitting there and told Helen about the night that she and Jenna sneaked into Jenna's parents' bedroom and snooped through Cynthia's important papers and found the birth certificate that led to Jenna running away to find her grandparents.

Cynthia covered her mouth and gasped. Megan looked terrified and said, "Oh no. I am so sorry!"

"Well, it just reminds me how wrong I was to keep her grandparents a secret," said Cynthia. "Kids need grandparents."

"What do you all think about the attacks on Israel? Have you been watching the news?" asked Jimmy.

"Oh yes," said Royal. "Did you see the Libyan soldiers with the bows and arrows in Egypt come down with that awful illness, and die right in front of our eyes?"

"We sure saw it," said Manda. "Dad was gagging and running to the bathroom."

"I always gag when someone starts barfing," said Jimmy.

"He's not any help when the kids are sick," said Kara. "I send him away or I have to clean up after him too."

"Well that was no mild virus," said Megan. "God struck them down and the whole world saw it!"

Jackson, Royal, and Harold shared with Jimmy's family why the invasion of Israel has become very personal to them because of their new Jewish friends who immigrated to Israel, right in the midst of all the turmoil.

"You must have had a near heart attack when you saw the baseball-size hail breaking windows and smashing people today," said Kara.

"We didn't see that," said Jackson. "Mom and Dad put us to work fixing dinner. But Joshua's family knew it was coming and were seeking shelter when we hung up."

"Well there are plenty more countries coming in the invasion," said Jimmy. "We saw many coming on horseback today. And they were trampling property and looting homes and businesses on their way. You know, I wish we could have met that family traveling to Israel. They were brave to go there in the midst of an invasion."

"What do you guys plan to do when you go home?" asked Jackson.

"We're going to start a Bible study and church service just like yours," said Megan. "And Manda and I are going to help."

"Yes," said Manda. "We're already studying our Bibles. But are we finally going to learn about the tribulation this Sunday and Wednesday?"

"We need to stop watching the television, and get those lessons completed," said Jackson.

"This is what I want to know about the tribulation," said Megan. "Will we get four years before it starts? I want to grow up and get married and maybe even become a mother."

"That's up to you," said Jackson. "But what if you get beheaded? What if you have to watch your husband and child get killed?"

"I will have forever to be with them with God and Jesus, and that's better than never knowing them," said Megan.

All of the adults were thoughtful for a few minutes, letting that sink in. Finally Royal said, "Megan, I'm amazed at your faith. I think that could happen."

"You trust God with your life and that of your family, just like it already happened," said Jackson.

"Well, I haven't even graduated yet, or met a good Christian guy," said Megan.

"When you're praying for that," said Royal, "pray for a nice, Christian wife for me, say about forty years old."

"I'll be on it," said Megan.

"There is one more thing I need to do, and to tell the truth, I'm not sure it's possible," said Jimmy. "My work friend who disappeared had a brother named Bobby. There was a note to himself to call Bobby and encourage him to come to faith in Jesus. I found Andy's phone and called Bobby and he told me that he wasn't interested. In fact, he told me not to bother him again."

"We are really new at being Christians, "said John. "But my mother prayed for years that our family would all become Christians, and here we are."

"Anyone who knew us would have said it was impossible," said Cynthia.

There were several around the table who murmured in agreement. "Well, I guess I'll try again," said Jimmy.

"Megan, I'm going to call you this week on my own cell phone, so I won't have to rely on that phone you gave Jenna," said Helen.

"Oh good." said Megan. "Let's do keep in touch."

"We need to get going," said Kara. "We have a puppy that Jimmy's aunt and uncle are watching, and I'm sure it needs a walk."

Chapter 22

After their New Jersey friends left the house, Jackson said, "Let's just watch the invasion for a half hour, and then we can prepare Sunday's sermon." The family agreed and they all got comfortable in front of the TV."

"This is Aiden Markel and my camera crew from CBS News in New York, and we are here in Lebanon at The Crossing, an area where Syrian, Iraqi, and Iranian soldiers overlap in the joint conquest of Israel. First we are listening to the Syrians. Anyone here speak English? What are your weapons and what are your plans of conquest?"

"I speak and I can tell you our weapons are soviet-made assault rifles, and believe me, we know how to use them. We are going to Israel and we will shoot up the place."

"Excuse me, but we are from Iran. We have the most superior weapons of war, purchased by money given to us from the United States' President Obama. We will demolish Israel!"

"But we Iraqis have agreed to go in and kill all who live in Israel, and not to hurt a single tree, lake, or field, or house. Men, women, children, babies, and old people are what we will be killing, and knives and clubs will do the job, considering there are thousands of us! You are breaking the deal of the entire coalition. What will you do with those Soviet rifles?"

"I will tell you what we will do with them!" Suddenly they were all shouting in Arabic and getting very angry. The reporter motioned for his camera crew to follow him to their van, where they jumped inside.

As they drove away, the cameraman captured the all-out battle going on, with many dropping to the ground and others swinging clubs, bats, and swords.

"I think we know how that will turn out," said Royal. "Back to my reading in Matthew."

"And I'm going back to the tribulation study," said Jackson. "If I don't get to it this week, we will lose half our visitors."

John asked, "What can I do?"

"I could really use a good map of the Middle East," said Jackson. "Could you work on that? And the bigger, the better."

"What can we do," asked Harold.

"Just check in with Angie, Ernie, Angie's sister Janene and the rest," said Jackson. "Joshua asked us to do that."

"We can do that," said Harold. "I think Angie is still mad at us, because we expect them to pay their own utilities, not to mention shoveling the walks and driveway."

"You are being very generous to Angie," said Jackson. "She doesn't face reality. She is a Jew, and yet she completely ignores God. And she has heard about Jesus."

"Angie doesn't wonder or care about the rapture and she thinks the tribulation is a conspiracy theory," said Harold.

"Well, let's don't listen to her whining about the outdoor work or the cost of utilities," said Cynthia. "We offered them the bargain of the century. But we can be good, caring neighbors, something we never were before."

"I guess that's the best we can do," said Jackson. "Joshua asked that we try to reach both of his sisters with the good news. After our encouraging Jimmy that he could reach Bobby, we need to have faith that Angie's family can be reached."

"Let's have the faith of Megan," said Helen.

"Yes," said Royal. "I like that. The faith of Megan. Can you picture me with a cute forty- year-old wife?"

"No!" said Jackson and Harold.

"Well Megan is praying for it, so I believe it's possible," said Royal. "Maybe I should get a new shirt. And a haircut!"

———

The family had a second church service with many more people attending, probably because of the sign outside the church! The sign read "Are you shocked at the invasion across the world? Attend Sunday to find out how it all ends and what comes next!" Jackson found an easy way to cover the end of the invasion. He simply said, "God wins and the Israelites stay safe. If you don't believe me, read Ezekiel 38 and 39. There will be so many dead bodies from the invasion in and around Israel that it will take seven months to bury them all."

Next Jackson spent part of the time discussing the antichrist and the deal he will make with Israel that actually marks the beginning of the tribulation. And since part of the deal the antichrist makes with Israel includes, not only their peace and safety, but also the ability to rebuild the temple, Jackson discussed the plans for the temple and the preparations the Jews have been making for years to accomplish that. Joshua had called him and shared all about a tour he took in Israel this week.

After Sunday's church service, Harold and Cynthia went home, very excited about all they are learning and something quite new to them, fellowship. As they were going in the house, they saw Ernie taking out the trash.

"You missed a good sermon today," said Harold. "I hope your family will soon join us for church services and Bible study on Wednesdays."

"Oh, that sounds good to me, but Angie isn't ready yet, so I'll wait a while," said Ernie. "But my sister-in-law and her two kids would like to go. Is there any chance they could go with you this Wednesday?"

"Two little kids?" asked Harold. "Does that include car seats?"

"Yes, the kids are little, so I'm sure they will need to take their car seats." said Ernie.

"We won't all fit in our car," said Harold. "I'll call my brother Royal. There's just one of him, so everyone can ride in his car. Tell your sister-in-law that he will pick them up at 6:00 pm on Wednesday. That will give Royal time to get the tech stuff done that he does for each worship service and Bible study."

The news reports coming from all over the Middle East were reporting huge numbers of casualties and even many regiments that were missing or not communicating. The Russians had many soldiers traveling on horseback, but the majority were coming by aircraft from all over Russia, Kazakhstan, Georgia, Belarus, Armenia, Kyrgyzstan, Moldova, and Tajikistan and were meeting at their airbase in Syria, with hundreds of thousands of soldiers, all carrying grenades, grenade launchers, assault rifles, and significant amounts of ammo.

Word reached Putin that many countries involved in this coalition had mass casualties from various places and unusual circumstances, and some of his advisors recommended pulling back. Putin laughed, and told them that since both the president and vice president of the United States disappeared, this is the perfect time to attack their precious Israel. He craved to attack Israel and take their wealth. The soldiers all landed at the airport and took off as a group. They stopped at the Israeli border to eat their rations and drink their water and pass around information about their attack.

The sky was an unusual color of purple, and the ground seemed to be quaking, not a lot, but just enough to make them very nervous and jittery. The commanders were calling the terrified soldiers superstitious for believing the stories of the fierce God of the Israelites. Suddenly there was an ear-splitting boom coming from a volcanic site that was considered extinct. Volcanic lava rained down on the entire area, destroying all of the Russian aircraft back at the Syrian base and all of the living things up to the border with Israel. News stations from Turkey, Egypt, and even Israel were reporting the carnage on their evening news.

A truck sped into the Ukraine from the border of Russia, and a man jumped out, shouting excitedly at what he had just witnessed inside Russia itself. Fires were breaking out in many government buildings, apartments, and houses. Many evil communists and their families were dying in the fires. But the Ukrainian man thought he should get the news of this out to someone.

For years he lived in the war zone where they had to endure relentless shelling from the Russians and hopeless poverty. The only help his family received was food packages and the message of Christianity from a wonderful mission. But the missionaries have not returned and there is a rumor going around that they disappeared. All he had left from them was a Bible in his own language and no food. He opened the Bible, that he never bothered to read, and noticed a phone number and a name Natasha. He pulled his phone out of his pocket and called the number.

"Is this Natasha?" the Ukrainian man asked.

"No. I'm sorry. Natasha disappeared. She's safe in heaven with Jesus now. I never listened to her message and now I'm sorry. Can I help you? I'm Natasha's sister Anita."

"I just don't know who to call and then I thought of Natasha and her mission team who delivered food and hope to us," said the man from Ukraine.

"Do you need food," asked Anita.

"Well, yes, I always need food," said the man. "But I just want the word to get out about what I saw in Russia. Places were on fire and no one was starting the fires! They were just bursting into flames on their own and people are dying. And I'm telling you, these were bad people. I know because of the way they treated me and others for years. And as I drove away and went uphill, I could see that the fires covered an area as far as my eyes could see."

Anita gave the man the address of the storage depot where Natasha went, with the hopes that there is food left there and that he finds it unlocked. And then Anita promised to get the word out about the Russian fires. Anita called a friend whose brother worked for a television station in America. An hour later, Anita saw the story on the six o'clock news and she was very relieved that she kept her promise to the man and it resulted in success.

Jackson and Royal sat with John and Helen watching the news. The lead story was about the Ukrainian man, running for his life from fires in Russia to his home in Ukraine. It told how the man drove up a high hill and looked back on miles and miles of a burning city in Russia. Members of the Ashcraft family looked at each other and marveled at the news. Jackson grabbed his Bible and it fell open at Ezekiel because he had read it so much lately. He turned to chapter 39, verse 6, and there it was.

"I will send fire on Magog and on those who live in safety in the coastlands, and they will know that I am the Lord."

"Well, I guess they do know to believe the word of the Lord now," said Royal. "So do you think these fires are burning up the families of those who sent the soldiers to Syria in the planes? They could be the families of those in charge, the leaders, and those in the government in Russia. I wonder if there are any others around the world who were encouraging the invasion of Israel, maybe even some in our own government, who are burning up."

The phone rang and it was Harold, asking to talk to Royal. "Hey Royal. I have a job for you to do. Remember Angie and Ernie next door, living in Cynthia's house? Well Angie's sister and two children want to attend Wednesday night's Bible study and they need a ride. We don't have room in our car for car seats and such. Can you go and get them? I told them you will be there at 6:00 pm to pick them up. That gives you plenty of time to get to the church and get set up."

"Oh I don't know Harold," said Royal. "I've always been afraid of children. How old are they?"

"I have no idea," said Harold. "But you just need to drive them. I'm sure their mother, Janene will take care of the kids. You will be doing a very good thing."

"I guess I'll do it," said Royal. "Joshua asked us to win his family over to the Lord by getting them to Bible study."

Wednesday night arrived and Royal went to pick up Janene and her kids. They were waiting outside on the driveway, and when Royal saw them he experienced feeling of panic.

"Hello there," said Royal. "My name is Royal. I don't think I met you the other night when we came over to talk to Joshua."

"Oh, I peeked in for a minute, but I spent most of that time reading to these two," said Janene. "This big girl is Angelica, and she's four. And this is Benjamin. You can call him Ben or Benjamin. And he is two."

"I haven't been around kids since I was a kid, so I don't even know how to talk to them," said Royal. "How about if I try and install the car seats and then you can put them in them."

"I don't sit in a car seat," said Angelica. "Mine is a booster!"

"Oh, sorry," said Royal. "See, I messed up already."

Janene helped Angelica get into the booster and fastened it. Then she ran around the car and helped Royal find the place to attach the car seat. "Can you lift Ben up into his seat?" asked Janene. "He's getting so heavy."

"You are kind of little," Royal said to Janene. He bent down to pick up Benjamin, who wrapped his little arms around Royal's neck. Then Royal lowered him into the seat and figured out how to fasten him in.

As they drove to the church, they chatted a little. "I hope you are enjoying living in Harold and Cynthia's house," said Royal.

"Not really," said Janene. "Oh, it's a beautiful house, but Angie's been such a pain. She expects Mom and Ernie's mom to pay for every bite we eat. And she has labeled me the maid. I have to cook and keep the kitchen spotless, and now she says I have to do everyone's laundry as well. I would love to find a nice little apartment and move out. My mom said she would move out too, and watch the kids so I can work."

"I just happen to have an apartment that I'm not using, but it's about a half hour away, since I worked in Cleveland," said Royal.

"Why aren't you living in your apartment?" asked Janene.

"On Thanksgiving Day, I witnessed 15 men, women, and children disappear right in front of my eyes," said Royal. "I didn't want to be alone after that, so I moved in with my mom and dad. Jackson and I were curious about the rapture, so neither one of us have gone back to work. We study the Bible every day and now we prepare for church and Bible study. Would you like to see my apartment?"

"How much does it cost a month?" asked Janene.

"I have to pay $350 per month," said Royal. "But I'm afraid he will raise it if you rent it. I've had the place for ten years and the new renters all pay more. If you like it, I'll just let you pay me if you decide to stay."

"Can we go look at it tomorrow?" asked Janene. "I can't wait to move out."

"Sure, I'll pick you up in the morning. Do you want your mom to go too?" asked Royal. "Can you fit in the backseat between the kids?"

"I think I can," said Janene. They arrived at the church.

Benjamin was sound asleep. Janene unfastened his seat belts, but he opened his eyes and said, "No. I want Woyal!" Janene tried to take him anyway and he started crying and resisting.

"It's ok," said Royal. "I'm sure we can figure out what to do when we get inside." So Royal carried the little boy inside, and he went back to sleep in his arms.

Inside the church, they went straight to Royal's computer area. Royal started it up and realized he can probably manage everything with the little boy in his arms. Janene pulled up two chairs for her and Angelica.

People came in and sat around the tables. Megan looked over at Helen and motioned for her to look at Royal. Helen was certainly surprised to see Royal sitting with a young woman, and even more surprised to see him holding a small child. She looked back at Megan and put her hands together, asking if that was the answer to her prayer, and Megan smiled and nodded her head yes.

Jackson moved to the front and began to speak, and as he spoke, he used a pointer and a huge map to show the countries across the world in the Middle East where things happened. "How many of you have been watching the news this week and the coverage of the Great Invasion of Israel? Most people raised their hands. What we are seeing is prophecy being fulfilled on national TV. It's happening exactly the way it was described in Ezekiel, chapters 38 and 39. The invaders have been hit with pestilence or some kind of plague and they turned on fellow invaders and killed each other with swords and rifles. Some others were rained on with heavy storms, baseball-sized hail, and burning Sulphur from a volcano. And even the evil people back home, rulers and family members, thinking they were watching in safety, were burned with fire. Tens of thousands of people who despise the people of Israel are dying. I don't know how long this Great Ezekiel Invasion of Israel will last. We may have as much as four years before the antichrist shows his evil, arrogant face, rises to power, and makes a deal with Israel, setting off the tribulation. Or it could happen any day."

"I made a new friend last week and his name is Joshua," said Jackson. "He and his family and a whole plane full of people, all Jews, just immigrated to Israel. Can you imagine going to Israel at a time like this, knowing that soldiers from all over the Middle East, were going there to kill every single person in Israel? The seven years of the tribulation are not going to be easy for the Jews in Israel or for us, here in the United States or any place else in the world. But I am excited for the Israelites, because very soon they are going to have their eyes opened, and they will believe that Jesus really is God's son, and that Jesus is eternal. Jesus came to earth as a baby, grew up and lived a completely sinless life. The Jews will soon believe that Jesus died on the cross for everyone's sins."

"Some time in the future, God is going to choose 144,000 of the people of Israel to be evangelists," said Jackson. "He is going to put a seal on their foreheads, and they are to go all over the world, teaching about Jesus and God's love for them. You can read about this in the seventh chapter of Revelation. You must know that the antichrist is not going to be happy about the 144,000 evangelists, and many of us will also be spreading the word. So we are going to have to be brave as we live as Christians and teach others, because the antichrist is probably going to have us killed."

"The apostle John, who wrote the book of Revelation, saw a vision of those of us who will be killed, and some of us could be who he saw. Read along with me beginning in Revelation 7:13."

> Then one of the elders asked me, "These in white robes-who are they, and where did they come from?"
>
> I answered, "Sir, you know,"
>
> And he said, "These are they who have come out of the great tribulation; they have washed their robes and made them white in the blood of the Lamb. Therefore,

"they are before the throne of God and serve him day and
night in his temple; and he who sits on the throne will shelter
them with his presence."

"And whatever you do, do not take the mark of the antichrist," said
Jackson. "Let's read about that in Revelation 13:16-18."

It also forced all people, great and small, rich and poor, free
and slave, to receive a mark on their right hands or on their
foreheads, so that they could not buy or sell unless they had
the mark, which is the name of the beast or the number of its
name. This calls for wisdom. Let the person who has insight
calculate the number of the beast, for it is the number of a
man. That number is 666.

"That is enough for us to think about tonight," said Jackson. "This has
certainly been quite a year. I'm not just talking about big events like
wildfires, hurricanes, and blizzards. I'm talking about the great
worldwide pandemic and then the riots in most of the big cities, and
the war against police and the actions to defund them. Such an unusual
year of craziness!"

"Next Sunday, we are going to learn about two people called the
witnesses, who are going to preach in Israel, and they are going to
annoy people all over the world, who don't want to believe in God or
obey him! Wait until Sunday, when we find out how people respond to
them. You won't believe it," said Jackson.

Jackson gave an invitation, and then said a closing prayer. Some
people left and some hung around to visit. Four more people were
baptized.

The next morning Jimmy, Kara, Megan, and Manda all went back to
their home in New Jersey, and they planned to start a Bible study.
Royal took Janene, her two kids and her mother to see his apartment
the next day, and they wanted to move in immediately. It wasn't very
long until Janene's mom was able to join Joshua's family in Israel, and
soon after that Royal and Janene were married, and Royal was a loving

husband and father. But before they were married, Janene came to believe in Jesus and put her faith in him. So the prayers of John Ashcraft's mother that all of her children and grandchildren become Christians continued to be answered!

James 5:16b The prayer of a righteous person is powerful and effective.

Also by Marleen Kunze

The First Ten Days

In a moment, life changes forever...

Imagine a time when millions of people from every country in the world disappear off the face of the earth. Such an event can actually happen "in the twinkling of an eye," according to I Corinthians 15:52 and I Thessalonians 4:17. Marleen Kunze considers the impact that disappearances can have on an ordinary middle-class American family in *The First Ten Days*. Matt Moses and his family investigate his missing sister's family, and in the process, they live in their house, drive their cars, eat their food, and spend their money.

As the Moses family live the life of their missing family, will they enjoy the easy life, will they wish they too had disappeared, or will they take up the mission of their relatives? What evil forces will the family face in a world that changes dramatically in just The *First Ten Days*?

Escape From Rome

No good deed goes unpunished…

Go back to a time in history when the Roman Empire controlled most of the world. One hundred thousand men spent their days at the Coliseum and other arenas watching vicious animal performances.

In Marleen Kunze's *Escape From Rome*, the adventure begins when the Coliseum manager's teenage sons witness a bloody performance and rescue a man about to be trampled and gored by rhinos. The fateful rescue angers the emperor and endangers the lives of Nolan's entire family.

Fleeing from the ruthless Emperor Domition, a handful of teenagers join the hunting team Nolan sends to Africa. As they trek around the Great Sea, they search for wild animals, and find survival and the truth about God.

Will the family escape from Rome and find the Christian faith they realize they are seeking? Or will they be captured by the the emperor's men and sent into the arena?

For sample chapters, and information about upcoming books visit **https://marleenkunze.com**.

www.ingramcontent.com/pod-product-compliance
Lightning Source LLC
Chambersburg PA
CBHW071808190726
48292CB00008B/2763